The Social Experiment

BY ANNA MAYLETT

The Social Experiment

Trilogy Christian Publishers A Wholly Owned Subsidiary of Trinity Broadcasting Network

2442 Michelle Drive Tustin, CA 92780

Rights Department, 2442 Michelle Drive, Tustin, CA 92780.

Trilogy Christian Publishing/TBN and colophon are trademarks of Trinity Broadcasting Network.

Cover design by: Trilogy

For information about special discounts for bulk purchases, please contact Trilogy Christian Publishing.

Manufactured in the United States of America

10 9 8 7 6 5 4 3 2 1

Library of Congress Cataloging-in-Publication Data is available.

ISBN: 978-1-68556-869-6

E-ISBN: 978-1-68556-870-2

Table of Contents

Preface

One dark and wintery night, snow came down so heavy that you could barely see the path in front of you; fog densely covered the ground, and the moon hid its light behind the dark clouds above; the aura it gave was scarcely seen. The branches of the trees bent with the heavy snow, and the wind howled like distant ghosts lurking about. One would think of haunting stories that would frighten a young child into its parents' bedroom. But this was the kind of night that took the lives of people that were very dear to the interesting persons of our story. No one could have predicted it as the snow just barely fell from the sky that morning, but weather often deceives us into thinking all will be right and then turns its wicked cheek to the side to show a more dangerous storm than we could ever have imagined.

The hugs and kisses that were given would have been much more sentimental if they knew they were their last. The rolling of eyes after being given instructions would never have occurred; the folding of arms, the look of the annoyance of having to stay with your sister would never have made an entrance in that house. But nothing prepared them for this great departure; nothing ever can, but it happens all the same, and now these two girls have no one but each other; as they hold each other tight, an officer explains the events that took place that evening.

Somehow hearing your parents' names used in the past tense makes things a whole lot worse.

The beloved parents of our story perished in a freezing river when their car skid off the road, and though first responders came quickly, and one gave his all to save them, all he could possibly give, even his own last breath, they were too late. The need to get back to their loved ones, the thought that they couldn't make it without them most likely drove these unfortunate people to their doom. They *had* to get back. There was no other option for them. A parent's heart is not perfect, but it's wide and deep with the affection they have for their children. The urge to shelter and protect never leaves them; they fear for their safety; they wonder if they did the right thing, taught them enough.

Life goes on when we don't want it to; life isn't a respecter of people; life doesn't care.

These daughters of the unfortunate, though just old enough to carry on without the need of parental supervision, must now carry on. The help they received from their friends and family, their church, their neighbors was greatly appreciated, and they got by; by God's good graces, they got by.

And though the years don't always help with grief, they can deaden the pain and, for the most part, you live your life again. Hopefully stronger and wiser than before.

Though we've only talked about one of the parties in this terrible incident, I must refrain from telling further, as I don't want to take away from the story I'm about to tell. So read on.

Chapter 1

Everybody has difficulties in life, and that is certain. We have our ups and our downs and everything in between. Sometimes we can have everything happen in the best possible way as if lady luck was always on our side and we didn't have to do or say anything to make it happen. Or maybe that was how it was for the other guy, and we just stand by and watch it happen, trying not to let jealousy control the fact that we have to work the hardest possible to get everything we can out of life.

And then there are the other times, tragic times when life gets the best of us, and all we do is suffer, and we wonder when we're going to stop feeling like we're drowning at the bottom of a freezing river as our air is cut off from our lungs.

But when those tragedies hit, we can choose to let them eat us to our core, consuming every part of our being until we don't even recognize ourselves anymore or confront them head-on.

Confronting our grief is not an easy task for anyone, no matter what age or walk of life they're going through. And not just grief alone, but depression and suffering usually follow not far behind. It's hard to move on when a loved one dies, especially one that was very close to you.

It takes time, months, years, an eternity to try and move on with your life, and sometimes that moving on is just taking it one day at a time, filling in the gaps of a monotonous life with something, anything that will take your mind off of the fact that you're all alone or feel that way: we tend to think we're all alone even when we're surrounded by people who love and care about us, but the feeling is still there, and one can't help but wonder if it will ever go away.

Our story begins with two unfortunate people that have to deal with the lemons that life throws at us, living the life after someone near and dear has passed on, trying to remind themselves to keep breathing and that somehow all will be okay, and as one becomes consumed by the weight he feels in his heart, drowning the sorrow that he feels and burying his feeling so that the world can't see the emptiness inside, the other filled her void in a small but adorable package. But don't be deceived; she may be using this package as a shield from the world.

We open on a cool autumn-like day in a small town of Indiana. It's the beginning of September, with the leaves beginning to fall off of the trees and the smells of them filling the air along with apple trees that line the groves of a neighboring farm; the sun burning bright is still quite warm, but the cool air deceives and one must dress in layers throughout the day with its unpredictability. Pumpkins are growing in patches and will soon be ready to be made into pies and bread. Friends and family all alike are getting ready for the upcoming holidays as students prepare for the new school year. It's a busy time of year here for all, but they wouldn't have it any other way.

As we stroll down the street toward town, we can see a business complex with several signs up above their windows, a big brick building that looks like townhouses lined up side by side, stairs leading up to each door; big letters fill in the windows of the business that is run there. Three doors down on the right is the sign that is especially important to our story, so we'll focus on it and read "Design it your way," a graphic design company built to help the consumers design and build their own business profiles with the help of a professional consultant.

Eliza Greene was a young woman of twenty-nine, short in build but strong in personality. Dark hair with eyes to match and freckles that cover her face and shoulders, she was attractive and very modest; her outward appearance matched the inward parts so that she was beautiful inside and out. But this also caused her to become an object that most men wanted to take out and get to know, namely Daren, a smooth-talking, very flirtatious man with an athletic build; his sandy hair was a little long, and he would constantly run his fingers through it, and his blue puppy eyes were the Achilles heel to any woman who looked into them; anyone with whom he wanted to be with would be his for as long as he wanted them, all but Eliza; she would always turn him down choosing to further her career and focus on her family rather than enjoy the romances of life, even for one night; it wasn't her style, to begin with.

She worked hard in the lowest position at this job to start out with cleaning and running small errands for all the high positions that were there, and before she knew it, she had worked her way up the ladder of that company in a few short years, becoming a project manager, though she had no formal degree from college; her hard work and determination were all she needed, and those around her were influenced by this.

As she was working on a project whose deadline was approaching rapidly, her employer walked into her office, a large, friendly man who was like a father figure to her, and sat at her desk. He normally came in with a smile on his face, singing or saying how beautiful it was outside, even if it was raining (because rain made the flowers grow), while adjusting his glasses. She had the highest respect for him. Today, though, he was looking very serious; it was very "out of character" for him, and this immediately threw red flags for Eliza.

"What's wrong?" she asked him. The worried tones matched the look of concern on her face as he approached her desk.

"Eliza, I've got some good news, and I've got some bad news. I'm glad you're sitting down because I don't know how you're going to handle this."

Eliza looked at him seriously and asked what was going on and if there was something she could do to help.

"The good news is that a promotion is coming up shortly, the one you've been hoping for, the one that will give you that raise you've been counting on. The bad news is that you don't qualify for it."

"What do you mean I don't qualify?" she asked surprisingly.

"I *mean*, it requires a college degree, and as far as I know, you are one class short of acquiring one."

"I've been with this company for six years and never needed a degree before; why now?"

"The new supervisor is pushing it; everyone has to have a degree of some kind; I don't understand why either, but I don't make the rules; I just have to enforce them. I want to help you out as much as possible, you know I do, and I think I can get you that promotion if you can take that final class and get your degree."

She thought for a moment.

"That shouldn't be too hard; it was only one semester that I had to drop out of. Could you work my hours around the class once I enroll?"

"That shouldn't be a problem. Once you get your class schedule, just forward it to me… I'm pulling for you, girly; I really want you to get this; you've earned it."

Eliza blushed and smiled shyly; she *had* worked hard for her job, but she never expected to be called out for it. She thanked her employer as he left the room and continued working on her project. When she got home, her sister asked her about her day as usual, and Eliza filled her in on what had transpired at the office as she pulled out her laptop to sign up for a semester class at the university.

"This looks like a good class," she said as she began filling out the form.

"Who's your professor?" her sister asked.

"Brent Collins. He seems to be a good teacher; he has some top ratings from some of his students on this other website."

"Well, whoever he is will have his hands full when you come into class."

"Thanks," Eliza said sarcastically as she submitted her form.

Hopefully, soon she'd acquire her degree and get the promotion; she truly needed it to accomplish her goal, and failure wasn't an option.

Brent Collins was a college professor at the university in town. He was tall with dark hair and lengthy in frame but strong; his features were very hard and serious. He didn't say much of anything outside of the classroom; more of an introvert, he liked to keep to himself and only opened up to people he knew. He didn't smile very often; he never really felt like it, but though he was rough on the outside, he was a very smart man, graduating at the head of his class at that very same university years back; his name was still on the basketball trophy in the glass case that was kept in the main hall there.

He had been in the town his whole life, though he hated to admit it; he would have rather traveled the world than be stuck here, but certain circumstances prohibited him from leaving, mainly because he was comfortable in his job and situation and afraid to see what was really out there, but he would tell you differently like he didn't have the funds or he wouldn't know where to start or something like that; he wasn't good at lying, but that didn't stop him from doing it to prohibit certain people from getting closer to him; as I've said, he was a hard man.

He spent his mornings teaching and his evenings at a party house that was inherited by his friend Katherine Sturges, a young realtor whom he went to college with, as well as with his other friends from his college days that shared the house, which I will tell you about by and by as you end up meeting his acquaintances later on.

The house they shared was Victorian style, yellow with white trim; ivy grew wildly up the side of the front porch as bushes lined up the front; pink carnations were spread throughout the yard and were covered with honeysuckles in the summer. Only one tree in the front yard, yet it would make a perfect climbing tree to whosoever owned the house many, many years before for its sturdiness of stature and strength in branches. A small driveway led up to this great house, which was always full of cars; so many cars, in fact, that most of them parked on the front lawn after the driveway had been full because there was no street parking on that road, which tore up the grass and took away the beautiful luster that this house once showed.

The house itself was magnificent inside; the foyer looked like an old church with a stained-glass window above the door; when the sun hit it at the right time of day, the most beautiful colors lit up the whole entryway of reds, greens, yellows, and blues. There were five bedrooms upstairs; Brent got his own while his friends shared the rest; eight people total live in this establishment of Katherine's; whether they are grateful to live there may be a different story, though it isn't quite the story we're telling, so we move on. The main level, as you have already heard some of the details, was truly beautiful; entering into the front door, on the left of the foyer was the living room, a great room really, with majestic green walls and wood trim throughout. The furniture that lined the walls was of the same period of the house, very antique and classy-looking.

On the opposite side of this living room was an office, which really wasn't used much, as Katherine wasn't the studious type; it was, however, used very much by her grandfather many years ago when he roamed this earth to author many historical novels, which were his pride and joy.

As you step straight from the front door, you will see the grand staircase that led upstairs, all wooden along with the banister, which was used as a quicker way downstairs by Katherine in her youthful days, but a more elegant entrance to her soirees now as she liked to glide down delicately. Going past that, you would get to the enlarged kitchen that included a bar area, which was very popular during these parties; of course, someone would always volunteer to mix drinks for the crowd.

And then a library with billiards was the last room before reaching the rear doors that led to the outside, which was Brent's favorite place to be during these raves for the solitude it had to offer, for no one wanted to be in that back room full of, what they would think, useless information. Brent wasn't always the best of company either, so he had that going for him.

All in all, the house was a great house to throw parties in, and Katherine never let an evening slip by without at least thirty people crowding the main level. She loved being a hostess and having all the attention drawn to her. Brent could care less about the crowded house; sometimes, he would stay in his room and get work done; other times, he was in the billiard room with his whisky in hand, playing a game or two on the pool table ignoring everyone around him. This was his life, that is, until he met Eliza.

Chapter 2

As the school year began, Brent walked into his full classroom; it was always full. In fact, not since his first year of teaching that class had he ever failed to fill every seat. In front of the whiteboard, which had his name written in large letters across it, he opened his class in the way that he always did: a greeting, expectations of the coming year, and a discussion of the great social experiment, a project he came up with to show the difference of social interactions between people, mainly between males and females. He had a different topic every year, but this year they would focus on "fun"; what is fun for one person may not be fun for all, and he was going to pick one of the students to help demonstrate this point. At the end of the experiment, they would show their findings to the rest of the class, and everyone would write a research paper about what was successful and what was not.

He wanted time to choose this partner, as he needed to get to know his students to be able to choose someone who would best fit the experiment.

Someone who was different, opposite from his own person. His motive being that he not only wanted to teach this student about the fundamentals of the topic of study but also of life. He found it a rewarding challenge to mold a young person's mind into whatever *he* wanted it to think, whatever decisions *he* wanted it to make; he was an idealist, and he wanted all his class to be one too, or in simpler terms, he wanted to create more people to be like himself. And he succeeded, too, for every student he chose was someone who was weak-minded and easily manipulated. And this is why he had received so much praise and admiration.

And so, this year being no different from the previous years, he kept a close eye out for that extraordinary student.

Although this year may have started the same as any other, especially for our delusional professor, it would be very different indeed as Eliza came in and sat down front row center, before the bell rang that day, in Brent's classroom. She put down her book bag on the floor next to her and pulled out her notebook and pen; as she looked around to the other students, she noticed that she was alone in this, for everyone was opening up laptops or on tablets, but she didn't let it phase her as she began to take notes in the lost art of shorthand.

Brent, as he taught, observed his students and their mannerisms.

His eyes wandered from student to student, making mental notes as he passed each one while he was teaching;

the students, being fully aware of what was going on, made themselves more presentable to our young professor, as they all wanted to be picked for said experiment.

He saw young men looking very studious, listening eagerly to his every word, and he saw young women, some flirtatiously batting their eyes to get some acknowledgment, of which Mr. Collins paid no attention, and some very nerd-like in appearance, not caring either way, for they knew they'd get good grades no matter what. And then he saw Eliza, and no words seemed to describe her to him, but he made a mental note that she was *different* from the rest of the class.

Our school year went on, and more observations were made, but his eyes kept falling on Eliza and her notebook. She, a woman much older than his other students, and her notes, which looked much like chicken scratches on that notebook paper; sometimes he paused next to her desk as he was teaching the class to watch her, which made Eliza very nervous, and she tried hard to not look up at him to avoid his piercing glance.

Every week for a couple of months, he watched her, making sure to pass by her desk a couple of times as he taught, pausing every so often to look down at her and her notebook and then moving forward. Eliza wasn't sure what was going on, but she tried very hard to ignore it.

One day as he came next to her, she finally did look up at him; his eyes were fixed onto hers, those serious eyes, those golden eyes. She began to breathe a bit heavier as sweat started to accumulate on her brow. The rest of the class became aware of this and began to stare as well at their teacher, wondering what their classmate had done that caused so much attention to be drawn to her. Mr. Collins, once he noticed that all eyes were on him, cleared his throat and made a gesture for everyone to go back to their own work, which they all did, including Eliza, while he went beyond her a few steps and then looked back at her. Have you ever felt that someone was watching you? Eliza did at that moment, and she looked back, but when she did, he quickly looked in another direction. So she went back to her notebook with a nervous sigh, still trying to calm her breathing down.

After watching her for those couple of months, he decided to choose her as his companion for the experiment. She had piqued his interest enough for the challenge, and what a lovely companion to have for the two weeks of the experiment. And although he did observe her for some time, he let his pride and his flesh get the better of him and, in haste, picked a partner he truly knew nothing about other than she did things differently and was attractive. Normally, he would've asked questions, especially of the other students, to find out more about them or request a paper about how they would handle a certain situation before making such a decision. But he became cocky and figured that, by now, he could change the pope if he came within a few feet of his classroom. Little did he know just what kind of a challenge his point of interest would be to him once he got to know her.

"Ms. Greene, will you come to the front, please?" he

said one cool November morning. She closed her notebook and slowly stood up, straightened her skirt, pulled down the bottom of her blouse, and walked to the front of the classroom to her professor's desk.

"I have been observing you for quite some time, and I would like you to join me in my little experiment. For two weeks, we will try to convince each other what our definition of fun is. The first week will be mine, and you shall have the next. We will begin around winter break, that is, if you won't be away for the holidays; if so, we'll try after the new year. I prefer to get this done as soon as possible. Will you be in town, Ms. Greene?"

"Yes, I will" was all she could say, nervous as she was about this whole matter.

"Good! I look forward to learning more about what you consider a 'good time,'" he said as he shook her hand; the bell rang, and all began to leave the classroom.

Eliza went back to her desk and put her notebook and pencil into her book bag and walked to the door. Brent watched her as she left, feeling very confident in his decision: this girl would be his greatest accomplishment yet!

Eliza went home with a lot on her mind; she wasn't expecting to be picked for this project, and she was feeling a bit apprehensive.

She entered into an apartment complex in her white '05 Chevy, which was running on its last leg. She climbed up the four flights of stairs and entered into her apartment, where she lived with her sister, Mary, nephew, Cody, and her brand-new brother-in-law, Philip. She put her book bag, which she always carried with her, down on the table as she walked into the kitchen where her sister was cooking dinner. Cody, a young boy of seven, was drawing so intently at the island in the middle of the kitchen that he hardly noticed his aunt's entrance.

"How was your day?" asked Mary. Cody looked up at his aunt from his work with a smile on his face.

"Oh, fine...I guess."

"You guess?" Mary said; she could always tell when Eliza wasn't acting like herself or out of sorts, which annoyed and yet pleased Eliza that someone knew her so well as that.

"Do you remember when I told you that my professor was acting weird? That he was always looking at me or stopping beside my desk while he taught?" Mary nodded. "Well, today, I was chosen to do that social experiment thing with him."

"What's a professor?" asked Cody.

"Auntie's teacher wants to do a special project with her," his mom explained and then looked back at Eliza. "How do you feel about this?"

"Nervous...anxious...I don't know..." was the reply.

Mary tried to calm her sister's fears with some reassuring words as Eliza walked toward the island Cody was at, but it was not until Eliza got a big hug from Cody that she began to finally calm down.

"What have you been working on?" Eliza asked Cody after a while of calming silence.

"Another c-comic of Astro Boy; this time, he's flying to help his favorite aunt at school."

"Sounds like an exciting adventure," she said. "One that I can't wait to read when you are done. Do you think Astro Boy can solve all my problems, Cody?"

"Of c-course! He can do anything if he puts his mind to it. That's what you always say!" He smiled and went back to his work. "I'll be done soon, and then you can read it!"

Eliza went over to her sister, who was draining the water out of the pot of spaghetti. "What have I gotten myself into?" she said with a nervous sigh. And then left to go to her room to breathe and contemplate.

Thanksgiving came with a little frost, very uncommon for this time of year, but Eliza and Cody loved it; frost meant snow was just around the corner, and there was nothing more that these two liked to do apart from drawing that made them so happy as to play in the snow, building snowmen and making snow angels or having a snowball fight. Once they had enough snow to build an igloo, which surprised Cody with how warm it was under a dome of compressed icy fluff; they were in that thing for hours before they went inside. Unfortunately, it was destroyed the next day by somebody they didn't know, but nothing can take away the memory they had while out there with it; Cody even drew a picture and hung it up, showing his pleasure in something so simple.

Eliza and Mary began the preparation of the turkey while Cody and Philip made hand turkeys out of construction paper. Not many people were coming over that day; Philip's parents and brother, Mary's coworker, and the pastor of their church were all that was expected.

Eliza began to set the table and left one seat empty like she did every year to put her parents' picture on the placemat in honor of the patriarchs that no longer sat among them.

"There, Dad and Mom, the prime seat at the table. You would've loved this feast. Mary did everything you trained her to do, Mom; she basted the turkey just like you did, and I made the stuffing, though it doesn't look quite like yours. I killed it with the mac and cheese, though! Dad, I know you would've loved spending time with Cody. He's just like you, very sure of himself and confident. Maybe he'll be a soldier like you." She wiped a tear from her eye and smiled. "I miss you both so very much. I hate spending the holidays without you here. I wish...I wish..." she couldn't continue as the tears increased, and she lost control of her emotions and cried heartily. Cody peeked into the dining room and saw his aunt; he had seen her do this before, almost every year that he'd been alive. He walked up to her and put his arms around her, "I love you, Auntie El," he whispered into her ear. She wrapped her arms around him in a strong embrace and said, "I love you too." Letting go slowly and smiling at him while wiping her eyes, she said, "You ready to eat?" His eyes grew wide. "Oh, yes!" His enthusiasm made her laugh as he almost leaped into the air; the pain began to cease, and her heart stopped aching. She was content with the little man that was before her, the only man she loved, the only man that she ever needed; why would she let anyone else into her life to compete with such a little man as this? "Cody, you are my heart."

"What does that mean?" he asked as he took his spot at the table right next to hers.

"It means that no one in this world has me like you do. You complete me."

"You complete me too! Now, can we eat?"

"Of course! Let's help Mom bring in the food." As this was said, Mary began bringing in loaded dishes and setting them on the table. Philip wasn't far behind her.

After the table was set, everyone gathered around and took their seats, held hands, and gave thanks for all of their blessings. The food was soon devoured, and small talk ensued. Mary was a great hostess to her guests, making sure they were all taken care of and comfortable having all that they needed. Eliza continued to sit with Cody, watching him draw what he was thankful for.

Philip's brother, Tim, sat down next to her and tried starting a conversation. "Enjoying your day?" he asked her.

"Yes, thank you," she answered, refusing to look up at him, concentrating more on Cody's drawing and hoping that he would go away.

"Your sister is a great cook," he continued. *He obviously*

can't take a hint, she thought.

"Yep." Frustration and a deep sigh involuntarily followed this answer.

"The mac and cheese was delicious. What kind of cheese was that?"

"Velveeta." Her short answers did nothing to discourage this extroverted man who could talk about everything and nothing at the same time. Eliza didn't like being around him; she didn't know how to leave conversations with him most of the time, and she hated to be rude. But today, she just wasn't having it. "Cody's drawing is almost done, and then I must help him hang it up in my room," she said coldly.

"Of course. I can help if you'd like—"

"No, thank you," she said abruptly, interrupting him. "I don't allow men in my room."

"Oh, it would be all right; we're practically family. Phil told me that you are a very busy woman with your work and now school, but you really must save some time for socializing and relaxing. I know of this great nightclub that would be perfect for you; it's hip and low-key, just your style. We could meet up sometime once you get off of work and talk business or Cody or whatever you would like. I know that I need to get a load off of my mind when the workday is done." *And then some,* she thought. *When is he ever going to stop talking?*

"All done!" Cody finally called out, interrupting Tim and calling Eliza from her thoughts back onto him; this was her chance to escape.

"Oh, good, well, it was nice talking to you, Tim, but Cody and I need to go now." They got up, but he rose too. "Please don't follow us."

"But—" he tried to say, but she hurried Cody off and shut the door and locked it behind her.

Cody was oblivious to the whole thing, only thinking about where he was going to hang up his masterpiece, but she took a deep breath and fell onto her bed; they stayed in there until all the guests left; she had no desire to draw any more attention to herself.

Meanwhile, Brent walked into the kitchen of the big house that was now abandoned of all the people who lived there and made himself a PB&J and glass of whiskey. "Happy Thanksgiving, Brent," he said sarcastically to himself. "Why don't you drink to your health? Why, thank you, I think I shall" and then took a big swig of the stuff. "Not what you remembered, is it? No, not really, but then again, nothing is anymore." He heaved a heavy sigh and walked over to the billiard room and racked up the balls. This was how he was going to spend his Thanksgiving— alone.

Chapter 3

Winter break came all too fast for Eliza, and day one of the experiment was afoot. December had made the air a bit colder, but snow hadn't started to fall yet. The leaves were all off the trees now, and all the shops in town had their Christmas decoration up and their colored lights shining bright. In the center of town stood a huge Christmas tree decorated with silver and gold glass balls, some small home-made ornaments from the youth throughout the years, and several twinkling lights dancing all around it with a gigantic star topping this masterpiece of holiday cheer; it became the pride of the town. Many a visitor or townsperson had come up to the tree and admired its beauty or made a wish for the upcoming year; many children would come up and try to touch one of the big ornaments that decorated its boughs. It was a thing of true beauty that Eliza admired every time she saw it.

Brent and Eliza exchanged numbers at the end of the last class before winter break. The next day, a Sunday, he texted her an address for her to meet him at, and she agreed to meet him there in the evening, for she already had plans that morning.

Eliza began to get ready to go out; she dressed in blue jeans, a black tank top, and a buffalo plaid button-down blouse over the top. She comes out of her room after inspecting her looks in the mirror and walks over to Cody, who was just finishing up a drawing at the coffee table in the living room; after seeing his aunt, Cody hands her his creation, which was a family picture of Mary, Philip, Eliza, and him; he was getting better with drawing faces, and it made Eliza smile at the progress he'd made over the years. *He's truly an artist now,* she thought as she studied the lines of the faces she was staring at.

"Here, take it with you," he told her. "That way, you'll always have us with you."

"Aw, you always know how to make me feel better, Cody. I love you," she said as she kissed his cheek. "And you constantly impress me with how well your drawing is coming. You are a true artist!" Cody smiled at the compliment. "It takes one to know one," he replied and ran down the hall into his room. Eliza went to the door and put the drawing in her book bag and then put it on and exited, not knowing what she was about to get herself into and feeling apprehension rise within her gut.

She arrived at the daunting Victorian house, which had music blaring and people everywhere. It was evident that whoever lived here was having a party. *But how could a college professor associate with such people?* she thought.

She approached the porch to people drinking and smoking, and she felt very uncomfortable but went inside anyway. She walked very slowly from the foyer down the hall (bumping into many people accidentally, for this house was packed from one end to the other). She passed the stairs and living room, all stuffed with people also. She could barely make out anyone's face in the crowd that surrounded her, but she was determined to find her professor, so she pressed on. She continued down the hall, going past the kitchen, and heard balls clanking together, which drew her attention to a room just beyond; as she peeked in, she saw a library with a billiard table in the center; only a few people were in this room so she took a few steps in just to get a breather from all the craziness she had just forged though, when who should happen to be playing pool but Mr. Collins himself with a glass of whisky in one hand and a cigarette in the other. He saw her come in but didn't make a sound, acknowledging her only by a nod once she looked in his direction; she slowly proceeded to approach him.

"Mr. Collins, here I am! What now?" she asked, trying to sound friendly and confident, even though her heart was beating so hard it felt like it would fly out of her chest.

"Go get yourself something to drink, Ms. Greene, and come back here," he said sternly, his features hard and grim, as if he wasn't enjoying himself and something was on his mind.

She looked at him, puzzled, but he ignored her and

went back to his game. Katherine entered the room with her drink in hand and made her way up to Brent, picking up a pool cue and brushing away a strand of blond hair from her face while saying how utterly boring everyone was this evening. I think I will take this opportunity to introduce you to our hostess and the owner of this establishment: Katherine Sturges wasn't someone whom you would call "a friend"; she, more or less, used you for whatever reason she needed at the time and then ditched you when she was done, but she did it with such grace and poise that you didn't know what was going on until after it was done, and to reject her would bring out a pity that touched your heart that, unless you had a strong backbone to say no, you would cave within minutes to this charmer. Her figure was curvy; she bore on her head blond hair, and the green within the brown of her eyes matched that of lightly colored leaves; her face had the beauty that youth can give, and her stature was confident in all she said and did, but the outward appearance says nothing about the heart and her inside did not match her outward beauty. The only reason residents would stay there in this house with her was for the free room and board. Brent was her go-to when no one else was available, and he knew it, but seeing as he didn't want any attachments either, it seemed to work out. *There are worse things that can be done,* he thought to himself.

Ethan, a man of thirty, who was sitting in the corner watching everything take place, offered to take Eliza to the bar to get something; he needed a refill anyway.

Once they left the room, Katherine came close to Brent and said, "She's a bit of a prick, don't you think?"

"I wouldn't say that," said he, not looking up at her but focusing on his next move.

"Why her?" questioned Katherine.

He paused and thought for a moment, then looked up and said, "She fascinates me for some odd reason. It may take a bit, but I think I can influence her just like the others."

"Is that *all* she is to you? You have no other motive than to treat her like the others?"

"Why, are you jealous?" he looked at her with a pleasant questionable smirk.

"No, I know what I am, and she's in no competition with me. I'll let you get your jollies out with this one, and then you'll get rid of her, and things will go back to normal; see, no jealousy! I don't see how someone so plain as she could catch your eye, though."

Brent shook his head just barely at the comparison that he had just heard and went back to his game.

Ethan and Eliza arrived at the bar, and he put his glass on the counter and asked for a refill of his beer. He looked at Eliza and offered her a chance to get a drink, but she refused, so he decided to start a conversation with her instead, "You are a very lucky young lady to be a part of Brent's project."

Eliza looks at him. "Why is that?"

"Because there is no one smarter than Brent! His theories and philosophies are so sophisticated. And he's a great teacher; you'll learn everything that he wants you to learn quickly," he said with a slur. "I know you will; you seem to be a very intelligent woman yourself. Much more intelligent than his other students who have done this experiment with him. And his theories and philosophies are first-rate, very modernized, I'd say."

"He expects to teach me his theories and philosophies? I thought we were supposed to show each other what our idea of fun was."

"Oh, yes, you'll learn all that he wants you to learn! But I can't imagine it being any fun. He loves to pick apart students' brains and tell them that what they believe is wrong, and then he teaches them the right way of thinking, I think," Ethan said, continuing with his drunken speech that now was becoming inaudible, but the words rang clear. So, his "project," as he liked to call it, wasn't to compare experiences at all but to influence people to believe the way *he* did. Well, she wasn't going to let him do that to her, no sir, she would only do what was expected of her from her fellow students, and her professor would soon learn that. She smiled wickedly, and Ethan, who was oblivious to everything, gave her a smile back. She ordered herself a beer, even though she never touched the stuff because of the smell, and then Ethan and she made their way back to the library and up to Brent.

"Ah, good! Now, why don't you sit over there and read this?" he said as he handed her a research paper that had his name on it, something he had written years back when he began teaching, and pointed to the chair in the corner that Ethan had claimed earlier that evening.

Eliza, speechless at the moment, looked at the cigarette in his mouth. "Oh, do you want one?" he asked her.

Ignoring his question, she said, "Mr. Collins, I thought you were supposed to show me a fun time."

"I am. This *is* fun, and you will learn all about the fun I am talking about once you read the wisdom that that paper holds and relax."

"What?" she said, her voice showing annoyed confusion.

"Yeah, you're too tense, Ms. Greene, loosen up a bit," he said as he lined up the six balls for the corner pocket.

"How can anyone loosen up here? It's way too crowded, smells horrible, and the music is deafening."

"Any other complaints?" he asked annoyingly, finally looking up at her.

"Yes! We're supposed to be having fun; this is not fun!" her voice was growing angrily. She always had a problem controlling her emotions, and this was no different.

Katherine rolled her eyes and sneered as she stood even closer to Brent. Eliza glanced up at her but then riveted her gaze back onto her professor.

"I'm having fun. Are you having fun, Kat?" he asked, not looking at her but keeping his eyes pierced onto Eliza.

"Immensely," Katherine replied, staring at Eliza as

well and putting her arm around Brent's shoulder.

"It seems to me that you're the only one determined to not have a good time." He continued, "Why don't you chug that beer, and we'll see what you're like once you've loosened up?"

"Might take more than one," Katherine whispered loudly to him as he began to chuckle.

Eliza had heard enough; she didn't like begin laughed at, and this was a new kind of bullying that she hadn't experienced before. She took the beer that she had in her hand and threw the contents in Mr. Collin's face as he stood there shocked, confused…and surprisingly amazed.

Kat was close enough to receive some of this spontaneous action and stomped off out of the room in disgust to wash herself off, exclaiming in rude tones how she couldn't wait for the prick to leave and how she'd never been thus treated in her own house, and so on and so forth.

"This is not what I signed up for!" she exclaimed loudly, almost yelling but still not quite.

"Well," he said, wiping his face of the liquid and being unusually calm. "Maybe you have been so deprived growing up that you're not sure what fun actually is."

Aghast at this remark, Eliza took Ethan's mug from his hands and chucked the contents of that onto Mr. Collin's face as well. She slammed the mug onto the pool table, right in front of the cue ball; it was a miracle that it didn't shatter into a million pieces.

"When you're really ready to start this 'experiment,' as you like to call it, let me know," she said, and she headed for the door.

Brent stood still, soaking wet and completely aggravated. *D--n, I guess I'll have to use a different approach with this one,* he said to himself.

Eliza stopped on the porch taking deep breaths, trying to control her anger, and sat on the front step; looking out at the pink and orange sunset, she pulled out Cody's picture from her book bag and looked at the lines of her family's faces. Ethan came over and sat next to her as she quickly put it back.

"You look like you need a smoke," he said as he pulled out a homemade rolled cigarette of questionable origins and put it in front of her face.

"No, thank you. I don't touch the stuff; not good for my constitution," she teases with a small smile. "Why do you have that?" she questioned him in wonder. She wasn't raised around this kind of environment and couldn't imagine anyone having a good time being here. All she could think of was curling up on the sofa with her warm brown knit blanket, a cup of tea, and drawing pad, anything that was far from where she actually was at this moment.

"This stuff is awesome; it makes you hallucinate to another place where you can forget all your troubles." He lit it and took a few puffs; Eliza was disgusted.

"There are other ways to take your troubles away, you

know, we could talk about what's..." She was cut off by Ethan vomiting by her feet.

"It makes you throw up too; I forgot about that one," he said and laid his head on Eliza's lap and passed out. Eliza rolled her eyes but patted his back anyway. *Oh, boy, what a night,* she thought to herself. She was so preoccupied with helping Ethan that she didn't notice Brent looking out of the living room window at her with his serious face and hard brow. Tomorrow he would begin a new technique, yes, it would all work out, and he would change her to his liking yet.

After a while, Eliza arrived home. "Hey, how did it... Whew! You smell of smoke and vomit; what happened?" Mary asked.

"You don't want to know" was all Eliza responded as she headed to her room, dragging her feet behind her, and closed the door, sinking into her bed; tears began forming in her eyes; she wasn't looking forward to tomorrow.

Chapter 4

The next morning, Brent decided to try his new technique. Standing in front of a whiteboard in his bedroom in the Victorian house, he had a list of ideas; number one was crossed out; that read "Read research paper." That wasn't going to work, so he decided to try number two, "Comedy club"; at least this way, it could look like they were having fun, but then he could converse with her afterward once she softened up a bit.

He texted the address to her but received a reply back that said she was working and would only be available to meet up in the evenings; he didn't mind this arrangement and agreed speedily, though later in the day, she began to doubt herself with this decision; meeting up with her professor in the evenings every day for the next two weeks didn't look very professional or ethical, but it was too late at that point; besides, she could take care of herself; she knew she could, and if worst came to worst, she knew half of the people in that town; all she had to do was holler for help, and anyone would come to her aid. "This will work," she kept saying over and over to herself, and later that day, she arrived at her destination.

"Why are we here?" Eliza asked as she walked up to Brent, who was standing in front of the club, shoulders slumped over a little; he was the picture of someone who was in complete ease of mind and body. Looks can be very deceiving, though; you may look calm and happy on the outside, but inwardly you can be in complete torment. Beware of this outer shell; it has set traps for many individuals that have come before you, a whited sepulcher filled with dead man's bones.

"You wanted a fun time, then I'll show you a fun time," he replied calmly.

"That's what I thought this whole 'experiment' was all about," she said with air quotations as she said the word "experiment."

They walked together into the club...half an hour later, Eliza was leading the way out of the building in fast, long strides.

"What?" Brent asked with a raised voice that sounded irritated. "That wasn't funny to you?"

"It was to you?" she replied in a huff. "He's putting down working women, the president, and our military, cursing every other word...this is funny to you?" her voice in a passion.

"Well, not when you put it like that, but you have to admit, some of his jokes were quite amusing."

"Not really!" she said as she headed to her car.

"Ms. Greene."

"What!" she replied sharply as she turned back around; the anger from another rotten evening was getting to her, and she really didn't want it to continue staying there.

"Where are you going?" he asked, hoping that he could stop her from leaving to discuss the topics that he found interesting to pick her brain, maybe even enlighten her a bit.

"Until you can come up with something more amusing, I'll be at my place," she said, annoyingly turning back towards her car.

"Wait!" he said quickly, and she turned back around. "At least take a walk with me so that we can discuss politics or maybe even religion."

"I don't think you really want to 'talk' with me about either of those... I think you have ulterior motives, but since I can't prove it, I'll give you the benefit of the doubt and listen to you for a little while longer; I don't have any other plans tonight anyway," she said with a sigh.

They walked a little down the street from the club, going towards the center of town. He wanted to try and bring up some topics but had a hard time figuring out how to begin, so he just walked silently in thought. Eliza, calming down now, would look at him from time to time in silence, waiting for him to begin but in vain, so she decided to ask her own questions, "How did you come up with the social experiment?"

"It was an idea that came to me in my senior year of

college; the professor of that university gave us a project of socializing with others who are different from us, and we were assigned a partner who was the most different after taking a short survey. Then we had to write a research paper after spending a week getting to know them, learning their mannerisms, their logic, and their habits, and about what those differences mean in a relationship. I was assigned Jennifer Trent, who now resides at that house that you dislike so much; I dare say she knows me better than I know myself sometimes because of that paper."

"Did you have a relationship with her after all that time?"

"A small one; we found that we were incompatible after a while... She is more of a sister to me than someone I could love; she then started to date a friend of mine, Kyle, and he ended up getting her to choose to be an elementary school teacher instead of the college professor she had intended on being when we were together...a mistake, I believe, but she seems to enjoy it."

"Why was it a mistake?"

"Because she should have stuck to her chosen profession, psychology; she could've influenced so many lives, helped so many people."

"You don't think she influences lives or helps people as an elementary school teacher?" she questioned with annoyance.

"She teaches a bunch of third-grade brats who will probably forget her name before the next school year, so, no, I don't think she influences them," he answered sarcastically.

"Wow!" Eliza said as she stopped walking.

"Wow what?" he asked and stopped too to look down at her.

"I never realized how conceited you actually were."

"Excuse me?" he said, also getting annoyed with where this conversation was going.

"You think you're something special just because you teach adults and have a title. Tell me, do you actually think of the wellbeing of your students or just how important you *think* your words are to them?"

Brent was speechless.

"I'll tell you what; a teacher influences no matter what age group or subject they teach. Being a teacher is one of the noblest professions, and I applaud the people who do it...especially the ones who decide to teach children, maybe even more so. Your friend is helping these young kids learn the things they'll need to get them through life, things that they'll never forget, skills that could help determine their destiny. I can't say the same for you..." she paused and took a long breath. She realized she was beginning to raise her voice, and perhaps she had gone too far, and after a long pause, she continued, "Look, I'm sorry for being so blunt, but I just couldn't help myself. This is something that has a lot of meaning to me. My sister says that I speak my mind too much; I guess she's right."

"It means a lot to me too, more than you will ever know." And they continued their walk.

As they reached the center of town, they saw the Christmas tree shining brightly, looking more beautiful than ever.

"I love this tree," Eliza said in a still, small voice. "It reminds me of happier times and peaceful memories."

"It is a pretty tree," Brent added, still thinking over what all was said. He was a meditator; words spoken into his ear would reside for a long time, rotating into every part of his being until he finally discarded it or was distracted by another word that was spoken.

They returned to where their cars were in front of the club in silence, no more talking, no more words, just complete and utter awkward silence. Everyone was coming out of the building and entering into the parking lot with them.

Eliza turned to Brent. "So what do we do tomorrow?" her voice was still quiet; she felt like a scolded puppy who got in trouble for digging into the house plants.

"Just come back to the house you were at before; I'll think of something," he said as he got into his car.

"Okay," said Eliza hesitantly; she realized that she had overstepped her bounds with their talk. She was always doing that; when would she learn to keep her big mouth shut? She was about to apologize when Brent shut his car door and drove off.

He went back to his little room and to that whiteboard

and crossed off number two with more gusto than he needed. Then, he went over to his desk to write down all that he had experienced that night. "Was she right?" was the first thing he wrote down; he had never had anyone challenge him before, and he didn't quite know how he felt about it. On one hand, he applauded her for her courage to speak up about her opinions and not back down, even if she was talking to an authority figure. On the other hand, he wanted to influence her, and after this talk, he figured that she might be harder to convince than his past students had been. After thinking for some time, he went back to the whiteboard and looked at number three and decided to give it a try; one way or another, he would get inside her brain. If parties and crude humor didn't work, then maybe this would.

Chapter 5

Eliza met Brent at his house again. She was still feeling bad about the previous night but perked up when she noticed that Brent didn't seem at all angry with her; he still had on his serious face, but it seemed to soften a little when he saw her and even looked as if he smiled a little. He was standing on the front porch leaning on the post as she approached him.

"So what are we going to do tonight?" she asked nervously but with a little confidence.

"A friend of mine is giving a lecture at the university tonight."

"Oh, what is he going to talk about?" she asked.

"Just some interesting topics that I think you'll find amusing," he replied.

"This isn't more 'Let's enlighten Eliza,' is it?"

He rolled his eyes as he walked over to his car, and she went back over to hers and followed him to the university.

Not many cars were in the parking lot, so finding a parking spot was pretty easy. Once they parked, they began to walk inside.

"It doesn't look like there are many people here," she said as they walked down the hall, but he ignored her; he didn't even look down at her and kept walking.

"Maybe he didn't advertise very well; I didn't see any signs that showed a special speaker was to be here tonight." He stayed quiet. "That must be it," she continued. Brent stopped, and she looked at him. "Whoever 'he' is, he could use a publicist. He may get a better audience if everyone knew about it; that's all I'm sayin'." He went towards a door and opened it, motioning for her to go in, which she did. There were only a handful of people there, and they all looked younger than her.

Brent came in after her, gently grabbed her arm, and led her to two empty seats near the front. He sat down and motioned for her to take the seat next to him.

A short, plump man walked into the room with a thin mustache above his upper lip and a pleasant expression on his face; he wasn't young but not very old either, perhaps in his late forties. His hair was balding, but he did nothing to hide it, and the dimples in his cheeks when he smiled lightened up the room.

He began with a question, "How does the brain comprehend the enlightenment of the world?" and then proceeded to talk for two hours with point after point of his theory. Eliza tried hard not to fall asleep, but this man seemed to know only three tones of his voice, and it slowly became a lullaby to her. She woke to Brent nudging her with his elbow. She looked up and saw that the man was writing on the whiteboard now, but it looked really blurry to her; she looked over at Brent, who was so entranced listening to this boring man. *How could he tell that she had fallen asleep anyway? Was he a mind reader?* She tried to concentrate again, but her mind began to wander, and all of a sudden, her eyes closed, and she was Alice looking for a white rabbit in a beautiful wonderland, and then she imagined being on a ship with a man with a black beard sailing the seven seas. Oh, how she loved reading Cody bedtime stories. Now, these stories seemed to become real, and they all starred her.

She was nudged once again, but she chose to ignore it and went back to a very handsome prince, who surprisingly looked a lot like her professor, who was about to kiss her. She was leaning in when her dream got interrupted again by Brent shaking her this time.

"What?" she asked with a yawn.

"The lecture is over; you're drooling, and I think you just called me 'your prince.'" She opened her eyes and looked around at a bunch of people staring at her, including the plump man with the thin mustache.

"Oh!" she said as she sat up quickly. "Great lecture," she said, trying to sound convincing.

"It looks like you were listening to something much more amusing," said the plump man as everyone laughed and went their own way.

"Ms. Greene, I want to introduce you to my friend, Professor John Brown."

"How do you do?" she said.

"Not as good as you are, my dear," John said as Eliza blushed. "Did you hear any of my lecture?"

"Honestly? No. I'm sorry, I really tried to listen, but I couldn't help falling asleep. No offense, but your topic is really boring," she replied.

John and Brent began to laugh. Eliza was puzzled.

"You're right, Brent, my lad; she is a piece of work," John said between laughs.

"Excuse me? A piece of work?" Eliza looked over at Brent.

"Well, you are," he said as the laughter stopped and his face became serious again.

"Well, I may be a piece of work, but at least I know how to have fun!" she teased, and his face softened again.

"That has yet to be determined. But I will admit that this wasn't exactly fun, but it is worth listening to," he said, and Eliza rolled her eyes.

"Brent, it was good seeing you again," John said as he shook Brent's hand. "And it's good to see that you're still up to your old tricks. Let me know how everything works out once it is all over with, all right?"

"You got it," Brent replied.

John looked again at Eliza. "Good night, fair maiden," he said with an overexaggerated bow and went to gather up his books at the front desk.

Brent stood up and gave a quiet laugh while holding out his hand to help Eliza up.

"I wasn't asleep," she said as they walked out of the room. "I was acting with my eyes closed."

"Acting?"

"Yes! Acting. I like to act sometimes, and I can concentrate better when my eyes are shut. That's all."

"Okay, Ms. Greene. Whatever you say. But…" and he paused and gave her a smile. "…but were you acting the role of a dog that you would drool like that?" and he gave another quiet laugh as he continued out of the building. Eliza tried to be annoyed with him, but she laughed as well. She liked being teased, and this was a good sign to her that he was opening up a little more, a feeling that she liked.

They were back outside into the cool night air when he asked her, "Are you hungry?"

"I could eat something," she replied. "But what's open at this time of night?"

Brent went into his car and pulled out an insulated bag from the front seat that he brought over to her and opened it.

"I brought some snacks just in case." And she looked inside the bag: she saw a bag of grapes, a pack of crackers, some cubed cheese, and a few chocolate chip cookies, which just happened to be her favorite kind.

They went over to the steps in front of the building they had just come out of and shared the snack Brent had brought.

Brent opened up and talked with Eliza for an hour about the interesting points of the lecture while they ate their snack.

"That sounds more interesting than your friend talking about it. He sounded so boring and had too much information to handle. All of which just mumbled together into sounds, not words."

"I guess I just have a way about putting things for people to understand it better."

"Or your voice makes any topic more interesting." Eliza stopped short, shocked at what just came out of her mouth and embarrassingly trying to fix what was said. "I mean…that…you have a way about saying things that is pleasant to hear. Umm, not that I like hearing your voice, though. I mean…" Brent held up his hand. "It's all right; I get the drift. And thank you, it's a nice compliment, even if it was all mumbled together."

Just then, a car pulled up across the street, and a man climbed out that Eliza immediately recognized as Daren from work. She quickly ducked behind Brent as he started to walk close to where they were sitting. Brent looked back at her, confused. "Are you okay?" he asked.

"Shhh. I don't want that man to see me." Brent looked

up and over to the man who had stopped to look at a message board near the university. "Who is he?"

"No one of importance."

"Well, he must be of some kind of importance to make you hide behind me."

"He's someone from work. Okay!"

"Oh. Ex-boyfriend?"

"No!" she exclaimed, sitting up quickly and then lowering her voice. "No, we're just coworkers. He's asked me out a few times, and I've told him that I'm always too busy. If he sees me here with you, he may get the wrong idea and assume that I am available to date and am just avoiding him."

"But you are avoiding him."

"I know I'm…" she sighed. "I know I'm avoiding him. It's just different, okay?"

She started packing up her things. "I need to go."

"No, don't go. Stay. I'm enjoying this conversation; it's much better than last night," he said, holding her arm as she was about to stand up.

"I'm sorry, but I need to go before I'm spotted. We'll meet again tomorrow. I look forward to seeing what else you're going to subject me to!" she teased with a smile.

She stood and, with a salute to him, walked over to her car and left. Brent sat a little while longer and stared over at the man that made Eliza so nervous. He noticed that this man was what women would find attractive, and it confused him why his student wasn't interested in him. What *did* she find attractive in a man? Why wouldn't she date? Then he remembered what she said about his voice and the way he explained things, and it made him smile.

The man in the distance walked away towards a separate building, and once he was out of sight, Brent cleaned up and took his pack back to his car and went home.

The next day while Eliza was in her office at work, she got an unexpected visit from Daren, who asked her when she found the time to start dating and then started to grill her on the man she went out with. Eliza wasn't taking any of it; she merely stated that it was none of his business and that he needed to go back to work; she wasn't about to tell Daren anything unless... (Okay, sometimes she could be a little devil when she wanted to be and decided to play into it.) She told Daren that the mystery man was her secret boyfriend and that they'd known each other since September (which was technically true, seeing that was when she and Mr. Collins first met anyway). But they were trying to keep the relationship a secret, especially from her sister, because she wouldn't approve.

Daren took it all in like the gullible man he was and didn't ask her out anymore; he did on occasion ask if she was still seeing her "man," with which she would smile and nod and then go back to her work. Oh, it was the best joke of all.

Chapter 6

Day four, and he still hadn't figured her out. *But that will all change tonight*, he thought. She met him at the old house again, and he decided that this time, they would go to the location together.

"Hi," he said.

"Hi!" she replied.

"Get in," he said as he opened the passenger side door of his modern SUV.

"What?" she asked, thinking she heard him wrong.

"Get...in, please!" he politely demanded with a smile.

She felt nervous all of a sudden; now, she wouldn't be able to freely leave when she felt uncomfortable, and she didn't really like that. She thought about mentioning something, but then he motioned for her to get in, and like a machine, she automatically did it without a second thought. He sensed that she wasn't all that sure about this, and it made him happy to make her apprehensive; truth being, he wasn't thinking of how wrong this looked to the outsider; he wasn't considering her feelings about any of this; all he wanted was to conquer at least one day, one conversation, of which he would feel much better than he felt in all of the past days; she would be forced to admit that he was superior and submit to his wit. Oh, naive professor.

He drove her to a different part of town that Eliza hadn't been to very often, and she didn't know what could possibly be here that would interest either one of them. He stopped in front of an old-fashioned, run-down movie house that looked as if it were closed a long time ago, with only a few lights on the front of the building actually working.

"What are you subjecting me to tonight?" Eliza questioned in a low voice.

"Well, you wanted to be amused…so I think I found a way to do it."

They exited the car and walked up to the box office. Brent, with long strides, paid for two tickets but didn't reveal what they were for, and Eliza followed slowly with her hands entering the opposite sleeve of her jacket so she could rub her bare arm, a sign that she was nervous.

"I haven't been here in years," he said as she caught up to him, and they entered into the building. "I hope it's still as good as I remember."

"Oh, boy," Eliza said under her breath.

They took their seats in the empty theatre near the back center; newsreels began to play from the 1950s and then a cartoon. Finally, the movie began, and to Eliza's surprise, *My Pal Trigger* started playing. She looked at Brent, puzzled. "What is this?" she whispered.

"My dad brought me here when I was really little," he said. "They only play old movies, mostly westerns. This was always my favorite to see, though."

"Huh!" was all she could say, amazed at him. Maybe he was actually starting to show a "fun" side after all.

When the movie ended, they stood up and started to head towards the exit. Eliza had a joyful smile on her face; she had never seen that movie before and enjoyed it very much. She was also relieved that this was all that her professor had planned and that it wasn't as bad as she was anticipating. But when she looked up at Brent to tell him how much she enjoyed herself, his features changed dramatically back to the hard and proud look they were before, except this time they were mixed with what looked like depression and anger. She began by saying, "I…" but he ignored it and began walking fast to leave the theatre; she, trying to keep up, followed behind until she reached his car, but he didn't stop and continued walking across the street; she had no other choice but to follow. His foot finally halted right outside of a drinking establishment. As she caught up, she said, "Do you always go to a bar of some kind, Mr. Collins?"

"I just need a drink right now," said he depressingly, not looking at her. She tried to get more information from him but in vain, for he refused to give any answers or acknowledge her now. All this began agitating Eliza, and she wasn't going to let him ruin the night for her like he did that first night.

They entered and sat in front of the bartender; Brent ordered his usual whiskey.

"And what does this pretty young lady want?" asked the kind, flirtatious bartender.

"Only a water," she replied.

"You sure?" he continued. "Because I can make you a very nice cocktail to go along with those looks."

Eliza smiled nervously and insisted that all that she wanted was the water she had asked for. Brent finally looked at her, with whiskey in hand, and offered her a swig, but she refused him too. She tried again to get him to open up, but he looked down at his drink again, not saying a word.

Well, forget this, she said to herself and stood up. She looked around the room; there wasn't much there, some tables and chairs, a small stage for when performers came, and a small dance floor. She examined the room again and again when suddenly she noticed out of the corner of her eye an opened door in the back near; what the flashing sign above said was "the bathroom." She journeyed there, leaving her depressed professor behind to drown his sorrows, as the saying goes.

She entered the room of the opened door and saw that it was the VIP room for exclusive parties, a couple of couches along the wall and a small table in the middle of them, and then, on the opposite side, she saw something that got her very excited, and she grinned.

If he won't have fun, then I will, she thought to herself.

Brent sat at the bar and stared at his glass, trying to forget all the memories that were surfacing around him, the sorrows that wouldn't leave him alone, and the brokenness that, he determined, would be his life from now on, no matter what happened. He now remembered why he didn't go to that theatre anymore; it was haunted, haunted by his past. He was so consumed by all of these thoughts that he was oblivious to the fact that he was now sitting at the bar top alone, but then he heard something; music began to play, and not the low humdrum stuff that was playing over the bar; this was upbeat...different. He stood and decided to investigate the noise; the bartender, who was drying glasses with a rag, was also intrigued and followed.

They listened and tried to follow the sound, slowly walking towards the back room and peeking inside. A small smirk started to form on Brent's mouth as he looked up at Eliza, who, having a microphone in hand, was singing and dancing to "Can't Stop the Moonlight" by LeAnn Rimes on a small stage. She didn't see him behind her, so focused on the words on the karaoke machine.

He heard her sing for the first time and determined that she had such a beautiful voice; he knew that he had never heard anyone sing like her before. He hadn't spent time with anyone like her before either. Had he suddenly started to feel again? Maybe something he hadn't felt in a long time? No! He was certain that he couldn't feel anything.

He took another long drink that burned all the way down his throat when he heard the bartender say beside him, "That karaoke machine hasn't been used in... I don't know how long, but it definitely has an angel singing on it tonight."

Brent nodded. "You're right," he guttered out and gave a heavy sigh.

He wished that he was so carefree like this girl, no... woman, in front of him.

He smiled again as Eliza swirled around and saw that she had an audience. But she didn't get embarrassed; she smiled and gave a deep curtsy as they applauded and then asked if anyone had a request. "You can sing anything your pretty little heart desires, young lady!" said the bartender.

"Well, maybe Mr. Collins will come up and sing a duet with me!" she said.

"Oh! I don't sing," he said, but the smile on his face kept getting bigger even though his heart was beating faster and his face began to flush.

"Oh, really, and how do you know? Have you ever sung like this before?"

"Well, no...but I can just tell that I'm not a good singer," and he tried to turn and leave, but Eliza rushed to his side and grabbed his arm.

"I'll be the judge of that," she said as she yanked him up on that small stage; he drank the last few drops of his drink and set his glass on the table next to the stage as she began to go through all the songs on the machine.

"Here's a good duet song," she said, and "I Got You Babe" by Sonny & Cher started to play over the speaker.

"Oh, no," cried Brent, but he sang along anyway.

They sang for a couple of hours straight, taking turns with each other; the bartender even got a few tries in; he would sing as Eliza would try and convince Brent to "Relax, loosen up and dance a little." Brent would smile as he remembered his conversation with her on that first night. He sometimes wished that he hadn't said some of those things now but knew you couldn't change the past, so why try? Brent, after all of this, was finally smiling and laughing; he couldn't remember the last time something like this ever happened, and he was enjoying himself.

He drove her back to her car and watched as she drove away until she disappeared into the night; the smile never left his face. Eliza felt the same as she walked up to the door of her apartment and entered; this was the best night of the week, and she was very much looking forward to tomorrow; finally, she had a good report to tell her sister and Cody!

Chapter 7

Day five went back to Brent examining her again, and she didn't understand why; she thought they had a fun time; at least, he looked like he was having fun, but maybe she was wrong; maybe he was just putting on a front with her, trying to deceive her to get her to let her guard down. *That must be it,* she thought. *But he seemed genuine, though.* It confused her so much.

The truth of the matter was that Brent did start to feel again that night, and it scared him. He wasn't about to let someone in so they could see the emptiness of his life, his hurt, his despair. Why tragic things happen to good people, he never understood, and he would never forget his past, never.

It was safer for him to treat Eliza like all of his past students and nothing more. He didn't want more friends; the friends he had were enough, and sometimes more than enough, and he wasn't about to look for a relationship, especially with a student. (Not that Eliza was looking for a relationship at all.)

He examined her, trying to get her to delve deep within herself so that he could see the innermost part of her being, but everything he brought up, every question he asked was always avoided by a smart-alike remark or with another question; she refused to give him a straight answer.

"What is your opinion on our government the way it is?" he would ask.

"All governments are different; some good, some bad. Why try to judge it now?" she would come back with, and he wouldn't know how to reply to it.

"Well, then, who do you think is a better president?"

"George Washington."

"No, I mean, within the past twenty years."

"Okay." And she acted like she was thinking, then concluded with, "I'll stick with George Washington."

"No, he died a long time ago," he would say, growing irritated.

"Really?" she replied, being facetious now. "Then how come I saw him at Mount Vernon a year ago?"

He just gave her a hard look while she smiled at him.

"That was an actor!" he retorted, and Eliza laughed, "Well, he was very convincing. I would definitely vote for him!"

She had gotten under his skin again, and she loved it.

On day six, the house was basically empty; many of the

people who stayed there had gone home for the holidays, including Katherine, which Eliza was very happy about because she got tired of being called a "prick" and "unsociable," which Katherine had no problem saying to Brent in front of Eliza's face.

Brent remained at the pool table, whiskey in hand. He discarded his cigarettes after a long debate with Eliza about his health; supposedly, he would die from them, and then who would benefit from his teachings, the worms? He determined that it was better to just not have one than to hear her go on and on about it again.

Ethan was there today reading a comic book in his corner seat as Eliza entered.

"Oh! It's nice to see you sober," she said to Ethan jokingly.

He looks up from his book. "Ha ha, yeah… I can go without drinking when I put my mind to it," he replied.

"What are you reading?"

"Captain Marvel…what a woman!" he said.

"Is that all you read?"

"No, I also read others, like The Hulk and Dr. Strange, but she's my favorite."

"I mean, do you read stuff other than comic books, like real textbooks or literature?" she asked quizzically.

"Not really," he replied. "Other books are boring…no pictures," he said with a teasing grin.

"What do you do then?"

"Brent calls me a professional student…I guess I am, though. I think I can squeeze a few more years of schooling out of my parents. It's easier than having to pick a career and go to work," he said with a chuckle, but even though it sounded like he was joking, Eliza couldn't help but feel sad by this statement; how someone could just go through life like that confused her; she had some personal friends who went through many years of college trying to find their place, but this guy's attitude was unacceptable. *His poor parents* was a foremost thought in her brain.

And from someone who had to put herself through school and work hard doing it, she found no pity for him: she had to drop out of college because life demanded it, but it was a choice that she would make again in a heartbeat.

She went to the bookshelf on the other side of the library and began looking at the books. Ethan, after a while of watching her, went to try and join her but tripped over the leg of the chair as he got up. He reached out to catch himself and ended up knocking over the table near him, which knocked off Eliza's book bag that was on it, which spilled the contents of said book bag in the process. Eliza ran over to him to help him up and clean up the mess on the floor.

"I'm so, so, so sorry…I guess I'm always clumsy, even when I'm sober," he said with a grin.

"That's okay! It was an accident, no damage done," she said with a reassuring smile to him.

Brent stood and watched all this transpire but became curious as Ethan inquired of one of the papers that he picked up for her on the floor. He began to move over to them.

"That's a picture my nephew, Cody, drew for me," said Eliza examining the picture being held up by Ethan.

"It's really good," replied Ethan looking at it again in awe. Brent moved next to him and took the picture to see.

"Yeah, he's got a very special place in my heart," she said.

"Why's that?" Brent finally asked.

Eliza looked at him for a few moments and then began her story.

"Because Cody is autistic," she began, getting their attention. "When I was thirteen, my parents died in a car accident. They were driving out in the snow and lost control of the car; they ended up in a river. First responders were there quickly but couldn't get them out quick enough; I heard one of them died trying. My sister and I were left to ourselves. She took care of me the best she could, sacrificing her own studies in the process. I was in my fourth year of college when she got pregnant. When she was six months along, the sonogram showed that her baby had infant traumatic brain injury or TBI; the doctor knew the baby would be born with a handicap. Her boyfriend at the time told her to abort, but she refused, and he left. Good riddance to him, too; I didn't like him much to begin with!

"Anyways, when Cody was born, I dropped everything to help my sister: I moved in, helped with doctor visits, diaper changes, midnight feedings...I never did finish college, which is why I'm taking your class now," she said as she motioned to Brent. "Cody has been my whole world. When he was two, Cody was diagnosed with autism. The doctor said that he would never keep up with normal kids, that he wouldn't even be able to write his name very well; I took it upon myself to prove him wrong. I schooled him myself, taught him how to read and write, and upon seeing how he held the pencil, I wondered if he could be taught to draw...so I taught him. Basic shapes at first, and then we moved on to more challenging things like buildings and people.

"Now he's seven years old, in regular school, and is able to keep up with the other kids and draws every day; I think he's even surpassed me. I'd do almost anything for him," she finished up, looking off into the distance with a tear in her eye.

Both Brent and Ethan look at her, amazed at her story, but that lasted only for a moment; Brent then remembered his own misery and decided that misery needed company.

"Is he why you don't date anyone or let anybody in?" he said, catching her off guard.

"What?" she asked, confused.

"You use him to shield you, don't you? You showed that the other day when you hid behind me at the school. You won't let anyone in because you're afraid of getting hurt or feeling that empty pain."

She looked at him with narrow, tear-stained eyes, shuttering from the shock of his outlook on what was said.

"I need to go." She packed up her bag and left feeling depressed and sad.

Brent smirked as she left, and Ethan looked up at him.

"Why did you do that?" he asked Brent.

"Do what?"

"Say those things to her."

"She needed to hear it."

"But—but that was cruel."

"You don't know what most of our conversations have been like. She doesn't hold back when it comes to my life; why should I hold back when it comes to hers?"

"She's a sweet, selfless woman—"

"Who needs to let go!" he chimed in.

"Sounds familiar," Ethan replied under his breath.

"Excuse me?"

"I said it sounds familiar. You shut yourself off from the world, won't get into any serious relationships, and brood in your anger. She, at least, will open up and love on *someone*, even if that someone is her nephew. Maybe she just doesn't want a boyfriend. What's so wrong with that?"

"You don't know her."

"Neither do you."

"I know her better than you do."

Ethan stopped and looked at Brent for a minute to think about what to say next.

"Maybe," he finally said after that moment of silence, building his courage. "Maybe you need to really get to know her. Maybe, just maybe, you might be able to talk with her and help her out of whatever *you* say she's hiding from."

Brent, astonished at the turn of the conversation, thought about this last statement and pondered if it might be a good idea. The woman did need some help, and he was her teacher, after all. He could provide the wisdom that she needed to hear and perhaps help open her mind in the process.

Chapter 8

Day seven arrived, a Saturday; they'd be able to spend the whole day together, and Brent knew this would be the last day he'd have control of the proceedings of the day.

Upon coming downstairs of the big house, he came across Kyle and Jennifer.

Kyle Sullivan, who Brent knew from his college days, was an accountant with dark skin and black hair. He was of medium build and was not very tall, only coming up to about Brent's chin, but he was a good soul, was very chill, and loved his girlfriend, Jennifer Trent, with all his heart. She, on the other hand, was spitfire contained in an average size frame, dark hair, and tanned features; she had no problem telling you her mind, and she didn't back down from a fight. She and Kyle worked well together; where she was passionate, he was supportive, and where he lacked in words, she was able to fill in with the right things to say. They were good for each other; Brent could see that on the first day that they met; he had no problem stepping aside, their love was something he had hoped to have had by now with someone else, but that was not the case.

"So last day for your turn, how's it going with the brainwashing?" asked Jennifer.

"Not like I planned, but soon enough," Brent said as he took a sip of coffee.

"Why don't you just have some fun for once...you know, actual fun?" she said.

He looked over at her with a critical eye.

"Yeah, you can't win them all," added Kyle.

"Well, I can still try," he replied.

"Oh, will you just give up!" Jennifer said dramatically. "The play has been played out. And I heard what you said to her yesterday, meanie butt, give her a rest, have fun; that's the whole reason for the experiment anyway, right? What are you going to do when you get back to class after the holidays and she gives you a bad report? Didn't think about that, did you? Well, I would be very careful if you ask me, Brent Collins!"

"She's got a point," chimed in her boyfriend.

"Okay, okay! I got enough from her this past week; I don't need it from you two too. What is this?" He looked for Kyle for sympathy. "Women sticking together?"

"No, it's more than that; it's 'I know you, and I'm trying to stop the madness!'"

"Fine then, no more brainwashing. No more experiment. I can't seem to be myself around people anymore."

"Don't have a pity party; be a man. Make the girl like you first, then try and talk to her," interposed Kyle.

"Kyle!" Jennifer yelled. "That is the opposite of what I'm trying to do here. He needs to lay off!"

Brent sipped his coffee and listened to the argument between his friends; they sounded like an old married couple, and they weren't even engaged yet. But as the heightened noise began to cease, he realized that all he and Eliza did whenever he brought up topics was argue, and he was beginning to regret it. Where did fun come in? He knew: when they talked of other things, their families and interests, and then sang karaoke at the bar when he didn't even want to at first.

He realized that he wanted to have another day of that, some actual fun. While looking at Kyle and Jennifer, he smiled; he knew exactly what to do. He grabbed his cell phone and dialed; Kyle and Jennifer had stopped arguing just in time to listen in.

"Hey, meet me at Jefferson Park at noon... Oh, it's a surprise...you'll see when you get there... No, I'm not subjecting you to something that will strangle your inner self to the point of despair, whatever that means... Okay, bye."

"Ha ha, I like her!" Jennifer said laughingly. "So do you know what you're going to do?"

"Yep," he answered. "I'm going to have some fun!"

Eliza arrived with five minutes to spare and looked around at the scenery: The trees were so pretty, all bare without their leaves, and the weather smelled of impending snow; the breezes were icy and crisp; she loved days like this. The little playground in the distance in front of her was deserted, and she started to walk on the path towards it. Upon reaching it, she noticed that she wasn't alone like she thought; someone was on the swings, just sitting there, so she went over and sat next to the familiar figure of Brent.

"So what questions are for today?" she asked, still a little peeved at him for the things that were said yesterday, but she tried her hardest to not let him get to her today. He'd ruined more than one evening for her, and she wasn't going to let it happen again. He may have won last night's conversation, but she was going to win today.

"No questions, just fun," he replied. She seemed a bit surprised, and he smiled because of it.

"What's the catch?" she asked quizzically.

"No catch. I understand that I was wrong to try and deceive you. You are too smart for my old tricks. So we are just going to enjoy some of my kind of fun. If that is okay." Eliza nodded slowly, still doubting that this was real. *Fool me once, shame on you, fool me twice...*she thought.

Brent stood and held out his hand for Eliza; she took it and stood also.

They began walking down the long winding path further into the woods down the trail.

"Mr. Collins?" she said after a while of walking.

"Yeah," he said as he looked at her.

"Why did you want to become a teacher?" she asked, trying to get him to open up more about himself.

"My mom was a teacher; I guess it's in my blood."

"She doesn't teach anymore?" she asked.

"Not unless she's teaching angels," he replied, which stopped Eliza in her tracks. "I'm sorry, I didn't..." she tried to say when Brent interrupted her:

"Don't be...she died giving birth to a younger sister who ended up dying a few days later, but I was too young to remember."

"May I ask what grade she taught?"

He hesitated a moment before continuing, remembering a previous conversation about Jennifer's teaching career, "She taught elementary school."

"Ah" was all Eliza said, though she wanted to say more but decided that it would just end with an argument, and she didn't want any more arguments with this man. Was she actually starting to learn him? This was odd.

"I know we talked about teaching before," he continued. "And I know what you want to say; I have personal feelings when it comes to my mom, and I have different opinions when it comes to my friends. My mom was an angel and always will be to me; she was perfect as a teacher, and it influenced me to want to be like her. Jennifer started out wanting to be a psychologist; that is why I got so upset when she changed her mind because I thought I knew her well enough, but I guess Kyle knew her more, and that didn't sit well with me. So, you see, I have nothing against teachers who teach young kids; I just got hot-tempered with the way you were putting your words, and I needed to defend myself, which didn't go over so well. Do you see now?"

"I do, and thank you for explaining this to me; I like these conversations better!"

"As do I," and they continued walking slowly, side by side.

The conversation continued as they walked together. They talked about the past and the present, even hopes of the future. Brent got to know Eliza more that day than any other day and started to like the person he was talking to. He learned her likes and dislikes, her greatest achievements, and her lowest moments; he saw how her relationship with Cody helped her overcome many obstacles in her life, and yet, he also confirmed that she chose to be alone and not pursue any relationship using her nephew as a front. He realized that she was probably too scared to be in a serious relationship because it could possibly take her away from the comforts of her life now. Change was a scary thing.

Brent, on the other hand, didn't talk all that much; he was a man of few words to begin with, and he liked hearing Eliza's voice as she expressed her emotions anyway. He would, on occasion, put his opinions in or mention something that he liked, and she would always praise him for his great idea or good taste.

They reached the end of the woods and kept following the trail; as they began to hear music, Eliza paused and looked at Brent with confusion.

"Come on!" was all he said with a nod in the direction they were going.

They got closer to a pavilion where a band was playing and went under the bleachers. "This is the best place to listen," he said. "More privacy."

"Who are they? I've never heard music like this before," she said

"Do you like it?" he asked

"Yes, actually. It's beautiful."

"They're called 'Flaming Strings,' my friend Kyle's band; they're great. I come here to listen to them from time to time. The other band members are Gordon, Chuck, and Sly. You'll get to meet them soon. "

They listened for quite a while to the instruments, jazz with a mix of soft rock and a hint of classical; it was a very unique style of music, which, when blended correctly, touched even the hardest of hearts. They listened until intermission, and then Brent took Eliza backstage to meet everyone. Eliza complimented them on their unique music style and continued a conversation with Jennifer, who was on her tablet looking up school projects from Pinterest to try on her class. Eliza gave her some ideas too.

Gordon came over to her and offered her a hotdog and some snacks that they had brought with them, which she gratefully accepted and began to eat her lunch. She saw that Brent also had a hotdog and was eating as well as he talked to Kyle.

Sly came to her next. "You can chill out here if you'd like and listen to the rest of the concert," he said with a very thick hippie accent. Eliza looked again at Brent, who smiled at her. "That would be great, thanks," she said. The group went back on stage; Jennifer went with them to watch from the wings and to leave the couple alone.

Brent and Eliza enjoyed their lunch to the eccentric sounds of the electric guitar, the beating drum, the soothing violin, and, of course, the hypnotic saxophone.

Once the food was consumed, Brent stood up and held out his hand for Eliza again. "Care to dance?" he asked.

"What?" she asked.

He looked down at his hand and then back at her, staring into those brown eyes.

"Would you like to dance?" he asked again, more professionally this time.

Eliza looked at his eyes as well; there was a happiness there that she hadn't seen before. She looked at his hand and smirked as she took it.

They danced a few dances in the little backstage area. The next song was much slower than the others, and they began a sort of waltz to it. He never took his eyes off of her and concluded that he might never quite figure this woman out, but that didn't really matter at the moment; he was having fun after a long time of just being.

He refused to let himself feel anything for her because she was a good, naive, and wholesome woman, and he felt that he could never have feelings for someone like that, or could he? He started to get confused on his actual feelings but didn't care at the moment, pushing it back in the furthermost part of his brain.

At the end of the concert, they walked back up the trail hand in hand to their cars in quiet. Brent broke the silence with, "Well, your week starts tomorrow."

"Yep," she said. "You better go home and get plenty of sleep. I need you at this address at nine thirty," she said as she handed him a piece of paper.

"AM?"

"Yep!" She said as she entered her car, "…you're going to church!" and drove off.

"But I haven't been to church in years!" he yelled after her, but in vain; she was gone.

Chapter 9

Early Sunday morning, while the sun was rising in the sky and the birds were chirping away their beautiful morning song, Brent arrived at Callaway Christian Church, wondering why he would dare think of going into it. He looked around at the parking lot; he looked at the side of the building and then looked at the gate that led to the cemetery that was just beyond. He hesitated a moment, took a deep breath, and then walked through the front door.

Instantly he was greeted by an older gentleman. *Gary, his name was Gary*, he thought. He honestly couldn't remember much at the moment.

He mentioned Eliza's name, and the old man showed him where she and her family usually sat in the sanctuary. He spotted her immediately, but she wasn't alone; he saw three other people sitting next to her: a man, a woman, and a small boy. He tried moving forward, but his legs wouldn't go; he tried again and yet again, but he couldn't go any further than the back row.

He seated himself in the back corner, slouching down so as to not be seen; well, he was as hidden as his tall stature would make him, but he couldn't hide from Eliza; she was looking for him every so often and, finally, spotted him. She wondered why he would be back there, wasn't he supposed to come up to her? She had come up to him on all the evenings prior to this one; wasn't it common courtesy to do the same? She motioned for him to come up to her, but he, just slightly, shook his head, so she made her way back to him. He looked very uncomfortable, kind of like the way she felt going into that old house of his, and he sat very still, almost like he was paralyzed. She sat down next to him and put her Bible between them so that he could see too, but he never looked down at it. His eyes were fixed ahead yet not at the pastor; he looked more at the lower part of the pulpit in front of the pastor like he saw a ghost.

To him, he did see a ghost, one that haunted his dreams and turned them into nightmares, the one that told him that he would forever be alone and broken, the one who kept telling him another drink would make everything better.

After service was over, Brent stood up very quickly and tried to get around Eliza, excusing himself. But Eliza wouldn't let him go.

"I would like you to meet my family, especially Cody; you can't go yet."

"I just really need to get out of here; we'll meet up again later; I promise," he said.

"Don't just run off; tell me what's going on. We can talk over lunch if you'd like…you must be very hungry; I know I am after service."

"I really don't want to eat anything, and I don't want to talk right now either; I just want to go…please understand," he said, almost begging.

She gave a sigh and said, "Okay," and let him past her. He took off walking in much quicker strides than when he first came in, leaving behind a concerned and worried Eliza.

Brent got into his car and began to tear up; he couldn't handle the emotions that were welling up inside of him. The last time he was in that church was when he was eighteen…at his father's funeral. A day he would never forget, though he drank just so that he could. He wiped his eyes and drove off to go home. Once there, he walked up the stairs to his room and shut the door.

He went over to his nightstand, sat on the floor, and opened the drawer, pulling out the contents within. Among all the mementos and papers, there was an old newspaper clipping; the headline read, "Car goes over embankment. First responder Eric Collins dies trying to save the lives of couple." He read further in the article to the couple's name and almost passed out when he read, "Col. Tom and Mary Anne Greene." So they were a part of the same story. He knew that the story that Eliza shared with Ethan and himself sounded too familiar, and this just cleared it. His dad died trying to save her parents; she, most likely, didn't know or realize. How old was she again? *Thirteen,* he thought she said.

He thought back to that day when an officer pulled up to his parents' house and knocked on the door. He remembered feeling like someone punched him in the gut when he heard his own dad's name along with the word perished. His memories followed that broken young man into the kitchen after the officer left and watched him pull out a bottle of whisky from the lower cabinet (his dad's brand) and pour himself his first glass of the stuff. And now, the burning sensation he felt as it climbed down his throat didn't stop him from pouring himself another and then another.

This was where it all started; this was the beginning of his downfall. He remembered going through college with a huge chip on his shoulder and keeping people at a distance so that he wouldn't get hurt again.

He remembered Ethan trying to help him get through his grief and then shutting him out, sometimes for weeks, so that he would finally understand that he didn't want any help.

Jennifer would try too; maybe it was why the relationship that they tried to have never worked; he had too much baggage, and she couldn't deal with a man who hid his feelings and refused to talk with her about them.

Katherine didn't care; all she wanted was a physical relationship, nothing more. That was something he could deal with.

But now, Eliza...when would it end? When would

people just leave him alone and let him continue to die slowly inside?

He put the paper back in the drawer, put his face in his hands, and cried for the first time in years.

Eliza called him a couple of hours later.

"Hey, are you okay?"

"Yeah, I'll be fine. I just had some stuff that I had to deal with, nothing important," he replied.

"Right...it sure seemed important."

"It wasn't, okay? Let's just forget it even happened."

She really didn't want to drop the topic, but seeing that it was going nowhere, she decided to change the subject.

"Do you want to meet up somewhere or do something?"

"In all honesty, I'm not really in the mood to do anything right now. So, if you don't mind, I'd like to just stay here and get some work done."

"And get your mind off of things, I suppose?" she answered, knowing that she would probably annoy him again.

"Perhaps...or maybe I just want to get some work done."

"Well, Mr. Collins, if you ever get done with your work and decide to stop moping around, I'll be at my house watching the football game and eating a hoagie... I'll make sure that I have one with your name on it if you'd like."

The thought sounded nice, and he was tempted, but he respectfully declined and, as politely as he could ever be, got off the phone with her.

This woman is going to be the death of me, he thought as he went over to his desk and began working on school papers that could've been put off.

Chapter 10

Day two of Eliza's week and Brent drove over to the address she texted him. He decided that he would give more of an effort today. Last night's rest had given him a new attitude, and he was ready for anything now.

He knocked on the door of a colonial-style house; it was blue with white trim. Bushes lined the front windows with different colored Christmas lights dancing around the glistening snow that was gently falling to the earth. A little overhang bent over the front door that was decorated with a wreath.

He heard kids shouting from inside; the door opened, and he got shot with a dart instantly.

"Hey, what did I tell you about darts in the house?" a familiar voice inside said.

"Sorry, Ms. Lizzy," said two boys that stood in front of Brent in unison.

Eliza showed up behind them with a baby on her hip and a spatula in her hand; the boys, upon seeing her, retreated to the den.

"Sorry, Mr. Collins, they know better."

"It's fine…and I think you can call me Brent now; we're not at school, and we've gotten to know each other pretty well. Who are they?" he asked.

"Well, Brent, they are our fun for tonight! I promised my friend Kelly that I'd watch her brood while she and her husband went out for their anniversary, a promise I made weeks ago, and you are going to help me babysit."

Brent put on a nervous smile; kids were not his forte, but he wasn't going to run away again like he did yesterday… he would stick it out, no matter what, even if it meant watching someone's brats for the evening.

He came into the house and closed the door behind him. He turned around to face Eliza, who handed him the baby, who began to fuss. "Here, take her while I finish making dinner. You'll find the others in that den back there," she said and motioned to the room on the back right, then she escaped into the kitchen. "Oh, and if she continues to fuss, you'll find her pacifier next to her sister in that room," she yelled.

"There's another one?" he said to the baby, holding it out in front of him. "How many of you guys are there?"

He followed the direction that he was shown and ended up in what looked like a TV room. It had a sofa and two armchairs, an entertainment center on one wall, and games on the shelves next to the TV. A young girl sat on the sofa near a lamp reading a book; she looked about the age of ten; the pacifier was next to her, and he reached for it and put it into the baby's mouth, which seemed to shut the little urchin up. The girl looked up at him, and he looked back at her; then he heard a crash and looked at the center of the room; the boys had knocked over a tower of blocks that was on the coffee table as they were wrestling on the floor.

"What was that?" a voice yelled from the kitchen.

"Nothing," the boys yelled back in unison and began to blame each other for the loud noise. Brent just stared for a while at them and then back at the girl on the couch who never took her eyes off of him. He gulped; now, he was uncomfortable.

"Dinner's ready!" Eliza said upon entering the den about fifteen minutes later. "Who's hungry?"

The boys took off past her to go to the dining room; the young girl, placing her book gently down on the end table, followed after them. Eliza took the baby from Brent, smiled, and left the room, and he followed.

They ate silently (as silently as you can eat with two crazy boys). Eliza was constantly reminding them to behave themselves and to stop shooting peas at each other and then made them clean up the floor and table after dinner was done, which they did while complaining that it wasn't their fault. The young girl cleaned the dishes without being asked and went back into the den to her book; the boys were not far behind her.

Eliza took the baby to bed; Brent followed, unknowingly

to her, and watched her. So gentle she was with this young child. So sweet her voice was to the lullaby she sang; a vintage type voice she had, something you would hear in movies of times past brought back to life by so few that you wonder if people still possess the talent; it seemed different than the way she sang karaoke a week past, calmer, softer. So tender was her affection to this babe that once was crying and now calm as can be.

Once the baby was asleep, Eliza backed up to leave, not looking behind her, and ended up backing into Brent, which startled her. She held her finger to her lips and ushered him out, closing the door behind them.

"You scared me!" she said, catching her breath. "I guess I should tell you who we're watching." They were making their way back to the den now. "The boys are Jackie and James; they can be a handful sometimes." *Sometimes!* Brent thought. *I think she's underestimating that!*

"The young girl is Carmen; she's very quiet and prefers to read. The baby is Grace." Brent nods.

"I know this is a little uncomfortable for you, but I do appreciate you being here to help me, and after a while, you will get used to them…maybe even play with them."

"Maybe," he said doubtfully, and they entered the den.

"Who wants to watch a movie?" she asked the kids.

"No, we want to build a rocket that will fly to the moon," said Jackie.

"Yeah, movies are boring anyway," added James.

"You didn't complain Friday when Mom put on *Cars* for you," stated Carmen.

"That's different; when Mom's here, we want to watch a movie, but when we have a babysitter, like Ms. Lizzy, we want to build a rocket!" Jackie added.

"Besides, her friend looks like he's never played with Legos in his life." Brent looked at the boy who was making a face at him.

"I played with Legos long before you were even born, young man," he said.

"Did they even have Legos back then?" asked the boy.

"I'm not that old!"

"Prove it then, build a rocket, I dare you!" said the young boy. That was it; Brent accepted the challenge and got on the floor with the two boys and started to build a rocket ship. Eliza sat next to Carmen and watched him play; she pulled out her sketch book from her brown cotton canvas bag and decided to draw the scene. It filled her with delight to see a grown man on the floor with kids playing.

After a while, Eliza was able to convince the boys to sit and watch a movie after they brushed their teeth and got in their pajamas. The kids all crowded around Brent on the sofa; James, who was no older than four, climbed on his lap; Jackie, who was seven, sat at his left, and Carmen, on his right; he was surrounded by kids. He looked over at Eliza, who was on the other side of the sofa, and she smiled back. Maybe kids weren't as bad as he thought.

By the time the movie ended, Kelly and her husband, Ted, had arrived. They walked into the den to see Carmen, Jackie, and James asleep on Brent, who was also asleep.

Kelly apologized for the delay, but Eliza assured her that everything was all right and that they had a lot of fun.

"How did *he* do?" Kelly said quietly, pointing to Brent.

"He was excellent, even though I don't think he's been around kids much. Thanks for allowing him to come over. I was worried that this would be too much for him at first, but he came through like a trooper," Eliza replied. "Whenever you need a babysitter again, don't hesitate to ask," she added.

"You're a good friend, Lizzy, and I'll keep that in mind," her friend replied.

Eliza went and woke up Brent, and between the four adults, they were able to get the kids to bed and the den cleaned up.

"That was more fun than I thought it would be," Brent said upon leaving the house with her. "Those boys are something else."

"I was hoping you'd have fun," she replied.

"So where to tomorrow?"

"How about the skating rink?"

"Really? You skate?"

"Not all the time," she replied. "But I do enjoy it when I go."

"All right then, see you there!" and they parted company.

Eliza went home happy and content; she had a great time and a night she would never forget as long as she lived. She carefully took out the picture from her sketch book and looked at it; she knew the perfect place to put it!

Brent went back to his lonely room; the smile on his face never faded. He lay on his bed and stared at the ceiling for a couple of minutes, deep in thought, thoughts that were occupied by Eliza and her generosity and love for others. Those kids were lucky to have her in their lives. He sat up and pulled out his notebook and continued into the night, writing all the events that happened that evening, leaving nothing out.

Chapter 11

The next evening came, and Brent met up with Eliza at the skating rink. They went up to the counter, got their skates, and made their way to the ice. Brent sped off as soon as he got on the ice, thinking that it was the same concept of riding a bike, you never forget, but he realized that he wasn't as graceful on the ice as he was when he was a teenager, and Eliza tried to keep from laughing but couldn't help it as he fell for the third time in front of her.

"Are you okay?" she asked him again.

"I'm all right, just need to break in these skates," he tried to say confidently.

"Are you sure it's the skates? Maybe it's the ice or the music that is throwing you off?" she replied with a teasing grin.

Brent would've been annoyed if he wasn't laughing along with her; he couldn't remember the last time he laughed so hard. She helped him up again and tried to teach him how to skate without falling, holding onto his hands while skating backward while he maintained his balance. They were doing well, too, until he got overconfident and tried to do a spin with her; they both ended up falling that time.

"Why don't we take a break and get something to eat? You look like you could use it!" she said to him, trying to get her balance again.

"No, I'm doing great! But if you need a break, I don't mind. Food sounds good," he panted, being out of breath.

They got some pizza at the snack shack that was a part of the rink.

"So, Eliza, how often do you skate?" he opened the conversation.

"Not as often as I would like. The last time I was here was probably a couple of years ago for Cody's fifth birthday party. He did as well as you are tonight, very wobbly," she teased. "I don't like coming alone. And no one else seems to want to come here with me. Then again, I haven't really asked anyone to come with me either. Who has the time, right? When was the last time you skated?" she asked him as they sat down.

"I don't know, maybe fifteen years ago or so...I think I was in high school," he said, thinking. "Yeah, Ethan and I came here. If I remember correctly, I didn't do well then either."

"You've been friends with Ethan ever since high school?" she asked.

"Yeah, best friends...actually, more than best friends,

he's like a brother to me. I guess that's why I look after him like a brother would. I don't want him to get hurt."

"That's understandable. He's a great guy, just needs some direction in life. I'm sure you'll help him in whatever he decides to finally do with himself."

"Whenever that happens, I'll be there," he said with a chuckle.

They ate for a little while when his attention was drawn to her book bag. "I have a couple of questions for you. Why do you always carry around your bag there?"

"It's more of a boredom bag. Whenever I get bored or think of something that I want to write down or such, I just go into this bag."

"What's in it?"

"Nosey, aren't you!" she retorted. "I'll leave it a mystery for right now, though I'm surprised that you asked. I thought you got a good look when Ethan spilled everything on the floor the other day."

He rolled his eyes at her. "What's your other question?" she continued.

"Why do you take notes in a notebook and not electronically? And how do you take notes? It looked like weird lines and not actual words in your notebook."

"Well, I take notes in shorthand; my mom had taught me how when I was growing up. And I like to take notes in a notebook; call me old-fashioned, but it gives me enjoyment to write stuff with my own hands."

"You can't type fast, can you?" he joked.

"Oh, I can type sixty-five words per minute, but I choose not to. I actually type up my notes when I get home and keep them on my laptop for future use."

"You impress me. You are so young and yet have such an older spirit about you. You're so open about your feelings and thoughts, yet you wouldn't give me straight answers when I was questioning you last week. You were so gentle with that baby you sang to sleep; by the way, you have a beautiful voice." Eliza began to blush. "And yet you could be stern when those boys were fighting with the peas."

"I do what I have to," she replied, a little embarrassed now.

"Well, I just wanted to say that I'm impressed." He took a drink of his water. "And I don't get impressed very easily." He looked at her more seriously now. Eliza looked at him too. Then things began to feel awkward, and she decided that it was time to move on. "Why don't you throw this trash away, and we get back on the ice?"

Once he got back, they decided to give skating another try, taking it slower this time around. They actually did a good job together. As they skated, they watched the other person and learned their weaknesses and strengths and would help and support the other when needed; doing this, they fell a lot less. But nothing is perfect, and they did have their times of falling and laughing all over again.

Brent went home that night with a huge smile on his

face and a laugh in his throat. He was actually having fun again, like the naive teenager years ago, before any responsibility, before any tragedy, before the loneliness of life crept in, and he liked that.

Chapter 12

Day four.

Eliza had called Brent and asked him to meet her at her apartment at seven—earlier that day.

He arrived promptly at seven, climbed up the four flights of stairs, and knocked on the door of seventeen B.

When the door opened, he was surprised to find that it wasn't Eliza but another woman at the door. This woman had dark curly hair and a fair complexion. Not the brown eyes of Eliza but green. She was shorter, a bit plumper, and she seemed to have an outgoing nature about her as she stood in front of him wearing an ugly Christmas sweater, jeans, and fuzzy socks, with a cup of eggnog in her hand.

"Uh, do I have the right place?" he asked her.

"Oh, you must be Eliza's professor! I'm Mary, her sister," she said with a smile on her face, and her hand extended. "Nice to meet yooouuu!" he said as he went to shake it and got pulled in.

Christmas music was playing, and the apartment was crowded with people, all wearing different ugly sweaters just like Mary's. He wasn't quite sure, but he thought that he had just walked into a Christmas party.

Mary ushered him into the living room and introduced him to some of her guests.

"And this is Eliza's professor, Mr. Collins. Mr. Collins, this is Tony Floyde and Tina Dunn; they're both teachers that go to our church. I'm sure you'll have plenty to talk about!" Mary said as she left him there to rejoin her husband on the sofa, who was talking to another couple.

He smiled at the couple there, and they tried to make small talk with him. He was courteous but couldn't help looking around the room for Eliza, though he couldn't seem to find her in that room, so he excused himself and went into the kitchen...no one.

The office? No.

The hall? Nope.

He headed back to the living room, not daring to go into the bedrooms in that hallway. Guests of all kinds came up and welcomed him and tried to get him to join whatever they were doing at that moment.

He was almost wrangled into a game of Monopoly by some young kids when he noticed a woman in that vary hallway that he had just left not long ago that he knew she wasn't there a minute ago. She, too, had on a sweater, just this one looked nicer than the others that he had seen, red with white snowflakes crocheted on it, and she also held a mug in her hand. He saw the smile of a friend, of Eliza, the woman he had been searching for. *She must have been in one of the rooms in the hallway and came out when she heard me*, he thought.

She made a motion for him to come, and she turned and walked back down the hallway; he followed not far behind her to the last door on the left.

"Where are you taking me?" he asked as they approached the door.

"My room," she answered and turned the knob.

Thoughts floated around in his brain of what all this could mean: He had never had such a relationship with a student before, but the thoughts were definitely there from time to time. Eliza was a beautiful woman, and they were getting closer, especially in their conversations; at least there were no more arguments! Could this really be happening? He was mixed on his emotions, fear or anticipation, anxiety or bliss; he wasn't quite sure. Perhaps it was a bit of all of them together. He stepped into the room, and as he began to walk towards the bed, she diverted towards the opposite side of the room. *Perhaps she needs to get ready,* he thought. But no, they were not alone, and Brent had to pause, realizing his thoughts were way off. He lifted his eyes to observe around him and saw that he was not in any normal room with bare painted walls but that these walls were covered with papers, almost like they were the wallpaper themselves; you could hardly find an empty spot. He looked closer at these papers and noticed they were drawings; drawings of places, sunsets, playgrounds, and people. He saw beauty, pain and joy, excitement and sorrow; it seemed that whatever this woman was feeling, she shed it onto paper and then hung it up to remind herself of it.

Among these papers, he recognized a scene, a moment in history that *he* was a part of: the night he helped her babysit. There he was on the floor playing with two boys building a rocket ship out of Legos; he couldn't help but smile; this was a good memory. He continued looking at pictures as he circled around the room, when, at once, he remembered whom he came in with and the fact that there was someone else that she was walking towards. He fixed his eyes on her now and the boy sitting at a desk near her; she crouched down next to him and whispered something in his ear. Brent slowly walked over towards her as she stood back up, looking at him. The little boy turned the chair around, and Brent looked at the face of a young, blonde-haired, blue-eyed boy with freckles lightly covering his cheeks.

"Hi! I'm Cody," the boy said in the politest way he could and extended his hand to shake with the professor. "You must be Auntie El's t-teacher," he added.

"Yes, I am," Brent answered.

All of a sudden, he noticed Cody's differences; he would flinch sometimes when he talked and spoke quickly, sometimes so quickly that he would stutter.

"You wanna see my c-comic book?" Cody asked as he took the book he was working on off the desk, handing it to Brent.

"*The Adventures of Astro Boy*, huh?" said Brent.

"Yeah! It's really me and all the adventures I have inside my head," Cody replied.

Brent looked at its page after page, astonished at how good the drawings were from such a young boy; it reminded him of the drawing Eliza had in her bag the other day.

"Did you draw all of these pictures?" he asked, pointing to the walls.

"No, those are Auntie El's." Brent looked at Eliza, amazed as she looked down in embarrassment. "My drawings are over here," the boy continued and pointed to the wall nearest the desk. "I want to be a great a-artist like Auntie El when I grow up!"

"You drew these?" Brent asked her.

"I told you I taught Cody to write and draw, remember?" He recalled the conversation she had with him and Ethan in the library of the old house. "I always try to keep a sketch pad with me so that I can draw whenever I feel inspired." She whispered closer to him, "One of the items in my book bag," and then she winked. He got the hint, looked at her, and silently chuckled.

"Is this your desk?" he asked Cody but still looking at Eliza.

"No, it's Auntie El's, but she lets me d-draw on here all the time!"

"She's a pretty special lady, isn't she?" he said, still staring at Eliza, who was starting to feel warm with anxiety; her smile left.

"Very special to me. Is she special to you?"

"Um..." Brent quickly looked at Cody, surprised. All of a sudden, he didn't know what to say to the boy. And Eliza found an opportunity and decided to turn the tables and make him feel nervous now. "Well, are you going to answer him?"

"I plead the fifth," he answered.

"W-What does that mean?" asked Cody.

"It means that teacher doesn't want to answer your question because he's afraid he'll say something that he doesn't want to admit."

"Why, you little..." But Brent was cut off by Mary, who had just walked in. "Are you going to hide in here all night? You should be out playing with the adults; we're about to start a game of charades."

"I don't like your parties or your party games," replied Eliza.

"I don't care what you like; come out and be sociable. Besides, it looks bad for both of you to be back here together with the door closed."

"But Cody is right here," and she put her hands on his shoulders.

"Cody, Max and Stan are playing Monopoly." That was all that needed to be said; Cody darted from the room with a flash and joined his friends in their game.

"See? Now, are you going to join us, or am I going to have to get tough?"

Eliza tried not to laugh to see her sister trying to portray a stern parent. She looked at Brent, who was so confused, and answered, "Even though I'd love to see you try to be tough with me, my professor's here, and I don't want to be rude, so…" and she motioned towards the door. "Lead the way."

They all followed Mary out to the living room, which was a little less crowded than it was previously; only a few couples remained as well as a couple of kids playing with Cody. Brent, Mary, Philip, and another couple were on one team, and Eliza and two other couples were on the other. Mary offered Brent a cup of eggnog, and he looked at Eliza and offered her some, "Nope, never touch the stuff," she said.

"Then what do you drink?" he asked, remembering how many times she had refused his offers.

"Hot chocolate, of course," she replied as she headed for the kitchen to make herself another cup. He then began drinking from his mug.

She came back towards the living room but was stopped at the entryway by Brent, who had just finished his eggnog and was about to put it into the sink.

"Hey!" Cody called out. "You're under the mistletoe!" Everyone looked over to them.

"You know that you have to k-kiss, right? That's what

mistletoe means. You know that t-that's what it means, don't you?" Cody added.

"Cody, you know that I don't believe in mistletoe and that I think your mom is silly for putting the stuff up every year."

"Oh, please, Auntie El, just do it this one time for me. Please?" he begged.

"You know that you have to do it now," added his mother.

"You're not helping," retorted Eliza. All of a sudden, everyone there was egging her on to kiss him. "It's tradition," said one. "It's mistletoe," claimed another. She looked over at Brent, who was looking at her; she shook her head in protest but eventually surrendered. She stooped and put her mug on the kitchen floor and then stood on her toes, yanked his shirt down so that he was at a proper height, and gave him a kiss.

He kissed in return, just a small one but just as sweet.

As this was transpiring, Eliza slowly reached up over her head to that mistletoe, and as she backed away from Brent, she yanked it from off the nail it was on and chucked it into the trash. "There, are you happy now?" she stated sarcastically.

"You're a party pooper, Elizabeth Greene," said her sister in jest. Brent continued into the kitchen and placed his mug into the sink, then paused and looked back at Eliza, who was still standing in the entryway talking to her sister. He took a few deep breaths to calm his fast-beating heart and then turned to join her, and then they both made their way back to the game of charades.

Something passed between them that night, and they began to see each other in a dangerous light: they were no longer teacher and student as they had been up to at that point but man and woman.

They played late into the night; Cody was put to bed, and Brent left after the last guest left with the promise of seeing each other on the morrow.

Chapter 13

Brent and Eliza met up at a nursing home the following evening with her church group. They were passing out gift bags to the elderly and singing Christmas carols. "Joy to the World" and "We Wish You a Merry Christmas" seemed to be favorites amongst everyone.

A lovely lady sitting in a chair by the window, who was looking gloomily when they first entered, began to perk up when she heard "O Little Town of Bethlehem"; she seemed to glow and then started to sing with the prettiest voice; it turned out she was an opera singer when she was younger and even sang at Carnegie Hall. The song itself reminded the woman of the sweetheart she once had in her youth who had proposed to her around Christmas time (he loved this song); she wished she had said yes but played coy instead with the hopes of a second proposal, but it didn't turn out that way, and he left her, feeling rejected. It was because of this that her Christmases were lonely and sad and that she was always all alone. She focused more on her career and became very famous at the time, but she never had a family whom she could love; of this, she felt regret. But now, she was changing her mind, giving life one more shot; even though she was in her twilight years, that made no difference now. It's funny how music can do that to people; just one song can have the strongest effect on them and influence their souls.

After all was done, Eliza headed over to an elderly gentleman who was sitting in front of a checkerboard and sat on the other side of the table. Brent came behind her and watched.

"This is my professor, Mr. Collins," she said to the gentleman across the table. "And this is Arthur," she continued to her professor.

After a few games and friendly conversation, the gentleman, Arthur, asked Eliza to get him some hot chocolate from the kitchen in the hopes that he could have a private conversation with this professor without interruption.

"Sure," she said to the older man. "Do you want anything, Brent?"

"No, I'm fine," he replied, and she made her way into the kitchen.

"So," he said after Eliza was out of earshot, "what are your intentions?"

"Excuse me?" replied Brent as he began to sit in the chair Eliza was just in. "I have no idea what…"

"Eliza is like a granddaughter to me," interrupted the gentleman. "I don't want to see her get hurt."

"Neither do I," replied Brent honestly.

Eliza began to come back out of the kitchen when she became distracted by a young girl who also wanted something sweet, so they headed back in together. The older gentleman noticed and took this time to find out more about Brent, asking him personal questions about his life.

"What do you do for a living?"

"I'm a professor at the university."

"Where do you live?"

"Near town." For every short question, Brent gave a short response.

He continued for a few more minutes, but seeing that this was getting nowhere fast, he changed the direction of the conversation to Eliza. "She's been through a lot, you know...both of those girls have..." he said and continued telling him about the tragedy of her parents.

He then proceeded to talk as if he'd known Brent all of his life, mentioning that he was there once in his life too, how he could have any woman he chose, but when it came to settling down, "The good girls are the ones we always choose," he said.

"I'm not looking to settle down any time soon; I assure you, sir. And you don't know me or what I've gone through myself, so please keep your opinions to yourself!" retorted Brent.

"Oh, but I do know you; I am you, professor. You may

say that you're never going to settle down, but that's something we always say until that one day comes when you least expect it, and you fall in love, then all you want to do is spend your life with that one special woman; she becomes your world. You think of her and only her. Her smile, her laugh, her smell, her touch...and her kiss." Brent, startled, looked over at him. "Your day is coming, my friend, and by your face, it's sooner than you think."

Brent sat and puzzled with his hand rubbing his chin, taking all of this in as Eliza returned with a mug in hand. He knew the older gentleman was wrong. He had to be wrong. He wasn't looking for a relationship. That would mean that he would have to feel again. But wasn't he already doing that all week? This was becoming very confusing.

"Did you guys find something to talk about while I was gone?" asked Eliza.

"Oh, yes! We got to know each other very well. Haven't we, professor?"

"Yes, I guess," Brent replied, still thinking.

"Well, I'm glad you're having fun, Brent. You see, I know how to have a good time," she teased and then turned to the gentleman. "Have you asked out Martha yet?"

"Oh, I'm waiting for the right time." Winking at Brent, he added, "She's a fox!"

Brent didn't know what to say or do at this point, thinking of the words the man, Arthur, had just said and comparing it to the past week and a half.

"Well, I wouldn't wait forever. If you're waiting on me for an approval, you already have it. I dare say you two would make a lovely couple."

"Well, thank you very much, ma'am. I'm planning a rendezvous with her tomorrow. I'll see if I can smooth talk my way into a date."

"Don't smooth talk; just be straightforward. Women don't like it when you beat around the bush. Just be honest."

"That's great advice!" said the gentleman looking again at Brent. "Don't you think, professor?"

And Brent nodded as he got the hint but wanted to ignore him as much as he could.

They stayed with the gentleman for a while before leaving with the others, yet Brent stayed quiet for the remainder of that conversation, too deep in thought to include himself in the context of what was being said with a man who assumed and projected his own ideas, which would turn out to be false in the end.

"Did you have fun tonight?" Eliza asked.

"Yes. Who was that man?"

"His name is Arthur Mcbee. He was a friend of my grandfather. They both served in WWII together; unfortunately, my grandfather never made it home, so Arthur became a second grandpa to me and Mary. I try to visit as often as I can, especially around the holidays.

Though I have a feeling he won't be available to see me if he begins a courtship with Ms. Martha," Eliza responded with a chuckle.

"He cares very much for you."

"I know. Always making sure I eat and take good care of myself. Did he say something to you to make you uncomfortable? You look more serious than normal."

"Oh, no! It's just that a man who was in a war and then taking care of the family of a comrade in arms is a very honorable thing to do. I'd like to learn more of his history if you have time."

"Oh, I could talk about him until I'm blue in the face," Eliza said. "He is such a spark of hope to all who talk to him. He helps everyone in this place; he even tries to cheer up old Ms. Weaver, who is sitting by the window. I'm surprised to see her smile and sing tonight; she came to stay early this year but has never smiled as far as I've seen. She's a lovely person. Grandpa Arthur is a good and great man, and I love him very much!"

"Was he ever married?"

"Yes, I was told that he was married once, though I don't know much about her. She died of cancer before he returned from the war; he doesn't like to talk about it much; she must have been very special to him, though; his face lights up every time he hears her name."

"What is her name?"

"Everleigh, isn't that pretty? He calls her Evy. For a long time, he hasn't really wanted to be around anyone else, but I'm glad that he's taking an interest in Ms. Martha; she's the sweetest."

As they entered into the parking lot, Brent walked Eliza over to her car.

"I'll see you tomorrow," she said to him. "Have a good night."

She proceeded to get inside the car, and Brent closed her door, then she drove away while he stood there a few moments watching.

He slowly walked over to his own car and paused. He wasn't one to get sentimental, but the way Eliza talked of the old man was getting to him; teary-eyed, he got in and started the vehicle.

As Brent drove down the road, all he could think about was what Arthur had told him. He did start to notice that he was thinking of Eliza more and that he dreamt of that mistletoe kiss the previous night. He smiled at the thought of it again but stopped himself. "No! I can't do this. It's too much to handle."

He returned home to an empty house and made his way to his room. He went over to the whiteboard and erased all the contents on it and then wrote "Why her?" at the top; he spent the next few hours writing another list, a list of destiny perhaps?

Chapter 14

Day six came. It was Christmas Eve; the experiment was supposed to be postponed until after Christmas, but much to Brent's surprise, Eliza didn't want to wait to finish up her week; the next place to meet up was at church for Christmas Eve service. The weather was the coldest yet, and snow started to accumulate onto the ground outside of the building. Brent went to service with Eliza and her family and actually sat with them this time. He even participated in the carols and clapped for Cody, who helped do a skit on the stage; he was the messenger boy telling everyone that the Savior had been born.

After service, they went back to the apartment for ham sandwiches and Rudolph the red-nosed reindeer. Cody loved Christmas Eve; it was his favorite night of the year; Eliza's too. Brent chuckled at how excited they seemed to get at everything they were doing that night: putting the stockings on the holder next to the tree (because they didn't have a fireplace), reading the Christmas story; even singing "Jingle Bells" while tidying up the living room was done with more excitement and enthusiasm.

Cody made his list for Santa and set it on the coffee table along with cookies and milk.

"I'm going to get more drawing pencils," he whispered to Brent, who was sitting on the sofa.

He said his bedtime prayers in the living room with his family that night.

"And please bless Momma and Philip, Auntie El and Teacher. And please let this Christmas be the best ever! Amen," he prayed and kissed everyone good night, even Brent, who he was becoming very fond of.

And then Mary walked him into his bedroom to tuck him into bed.

Eliza came and sat next to Brent on the sofa and said as she leaned towards him, "And a new notebook; he forgot that he's on his last few pages. I find it interesting that a boy of his age only wants drawing pencils and notebooks for Christmas."

"Like you've said, he's very special," he said.

"That he is, my special angel. I don't know where I would be without him," she said as Mary came over to them with a bedsheet, pillow, and blanket.

"Cody insists that you spend the night; he'll be disappointed if he doesn't see you in the morning," said Mary, and she put the sheet, pillow, and blanket on the sofa next to him.

"I really should be going," he replied, starting to stand.

"No, stay. Please?" asked Eliza in a sweet manner. "It would mean a lot to Cody; he's really starting to like you."

"No, I can't. This is a family thing, and I don't want to impose."

"It's not an imposition; it's an experiment, remember? And I won't take no for an answer!"

Brent thought for a moment and then surrendered. He kind of liked the idea of spending the holidays with someone other than himself for once, and Eliza was so friendly and nice to him; it was irresistible. Though he had his reservations, he figured that there would be no harm in one night.

"Okay...for Cody, I'll stay," he replied and sat back down next to her.

Mary rolled her eyes and smiled. "Goodnight, you two." And then left with Philip, who was coming out of the kitchen after doing the dishes.

Brent and Eliza got up, and she started preparing the sofa with the sheet and put the pillow on one of the ends, then laid the blanket on top. Brent sat down again once she was done, and she sat next to him as they were before.

"Do you have any traditions that you and your family did when you were younger?" she asked him.

"Nothing different from what other families do, I guess...except—" he said with a pause.

"Go on!" she said impatiently.

"When I was a teenager, my dad and I would play Clue

until midnight, and then we'd say a prayer wishing my mom and sister a very merry Christmas."

"That's sweet! Where's your dad now?" she asked.

"He died many years ago when I was eighteen."

"I'm sorry," Eliza sympathetically said. "Do you have any family that you spend Christmas with? Aunts, uncles, cousins?"

"No, I usually spend it alone. I spend all of my holidays alone. But it's not a bad thing. I don't have to fight over food or worry about saying things that will start an argument. I do go over to the graveyard sometimes and will talk, if you can call it talk, to my dad, but for the most part...yeah."

"It sounds lonely. You are always welcome here," she said and reached for his hand for comfort but ended up stirring emotions instead; Brent teared up and decided, after all her generosity, that he should probably open up to her about their shared past.

"I need to tell you something that I found out earlier this week: You see, my dad was a first responder, and I was very proud—*am* still—very proud of him. We were supposed to see a movie in that old movie house when he got a call that a car had slipped off of the road into a river next to the old bridge one cold December evening."

Eliza gasped. "My parents? ...Your Dad was the man who tried to save my parents?"

"I recognized your story last week when you were telling Ethan; it matched my own, and then I looked it up in old newspapers and found it to be true," Brent continued. "I was amazed how you could move on like you did, become the selfless woman you are after such a tragedy at such a young age; most people that I have seen go through such an event usually harbor ill feelings or can't seem to get over the grief, but you have. I love to see you with Cody; you've done so much for him…"

"He's done so much for me," she interrupted. "I can't imagine my life without him in it."

"You're a good woman, Eliza Greene," he said as he leaned closer to her. She didn't know why, but she began to lean into him too. He reached up and smoothed the loose hairs away from her face and put them behind her ear, and while holding her there, letting loose all the pent-up emotions that had been straining his heart for a while now, enclosed his lips onto hers. To his pleasant surprise, she didn't pull away but instead kissed him back softly and gently. They broke just slightly to gaze into each other's eyes and then began to kiss again, with intensity growing every minute. Eliza knew in the back of her mind that it was wrong. She knew she should probably stop, but it felt so good. He pulled her in closer and just held her there, refusing to stop the passion, and she melted into his arms.

All of a sudden, they heard a child calling from the room down the hall, "Auntie El, Auntie El, help! The pirates!"

Eliza broke away at that moment, out of breath, and said very softly, "That's Cody," and a few deep breaths later, "I've got to go."

"No, don't go…please," he said while she stood up and began to pass him. He tried to gently grab her arm and repeated, "Please." She made eye contact and had a look of sorrowful agony but didn't obey his request. She started to feel guilty for what had just happened and was thankful for what felt like a divine interruption.

She had overstepped her bounds; he was her teacher; she was his student. She couldn't fall in love with her teacher. She wouldn't! She exited the living room and headed for Cody's room down the hall.

Brent lay on the sofa alone, staring at the ceiling, thinking of Eliza while she lay in Cody's bed next to him while he slept (he must have had a bad dream, for he was asleep again once she entered the door). All she could think of was Brent. The two suffered a sleepless night, thinking of all that had transpired between them. One thought of the sin and tried to resolve what to do to extricate herself from the problem, and the other, with the hope of the future before him, lay with a smile, thinking of the beauty of it all.

Chapter 15

Day seven, Christmas Day.

Cody rushed into the living room, shouting, "It's Christmas! It's Christmas!" which woke up Brent, who had finally drifted off to sleep about an hour ago.

Mary, Philip, and Eliza came in together, and Mary put a mug of coffee on the table in front of Brent. He sat up, looking at Eliza, who had just passed in front of him, and once he made eye contact with her, he looked down at the empty spot on the sofa next to him, hoping that she'd sit there, but she gently shook her head and sat on the floor next to the tree with Cody, her eyes bent towards the hardwood floor. Philip sat next to Brent instead, and Mary took a seat in the chair next to him.

"Can I go first?" asked Cody; his mom nodded in approval.

"What did you get, Cody?" asked Brent as he picked up the mug and drank from it while Cody picked up some presents.

"Oh, he likes to give out his presents first," said Mary.

Cody then began to pass out the sloppily wrapped tubes, one to everyone, including Brent.

Everyone began to unwrap their presents after they had received them from Cody; Mary got a drawing of the Arc de Triomphe (her favorite building in Paris); she gave him kiss after kiss and said, "Thank you, Cody, you know me so well!"

"Is it better than the one I drew for you last year?" he asked (Cody had been drawing his mom the same picture every year since he was four).

"Yes, your drawing is improving so much!" she replied.

She went and replaced the one on the fridge that had stayed there for the whole of the year and then put the old picture on the kitchen table with the intent of putting it in the scrapbook that she had started when Cody was a baby (the same place she had all of the other drawings in). She loved filling it in with his masterpieces, and then she would take pictures of him and paste them together on the pages.

Philip opened his and found a portrait of Cody and himself inside.

"I thought you would like it for your office," said Cody.

"Thanks, little man," he said with a tear in his eye, which he quickly wiped away. This was Cody's first drawing of the two of them together, just the two of them, and he felt as if Cody was finally accepting him as a father. It was something that he had hoped Cody would do for the last three years that he and his mom had been together. Cody may have said that they were family or even called him Dad on occasion, but this was more; this was special, and he gave this little artist a great big bear hug followed by a tickling under Cody's arms that he knew the kid couldn't resist.

Brent opened his next; it was a comic book entitled *Astro Boy and the Teacher*.

"Now we can go on adventures together!" Cody said very excitedly.

Brent smiled. "Thank you, Cody...I can't wait to read this and see where we end up." He opened it and read only a couple of pages before placing it on the table in front of him. He didn't expect to get anything, and gratitude was shown on his features as Cody rushed a hug on him without him knowing. "Thank you, Cody," he said again.

"You're welcome," the boy replied and then got down and looked at his aunt.

Eliza sat very still, staring at the picture in front of her with a blank expression.

"What did you get?" asked her sister. Eliza looked up as if she had seen a ghost; she stood up and handed the picture to Mary, who looked back at her curiously. Eliza walked back over to Cody and gave him a big hug and thanked him for the picture; though her voice sounded a bit shaky, she tried to cover it up. Mary looked at the picture and then back at Eliza with those big green eyes in concern and handed the picture to her husband, who also was asking what all of this was about.

He took it and put it between him and Brent so that they both could get a good look at it, and there, right in front of their faces, was a beautifully drawn picture of Eliza and Brent together, smiling as though they belonged with each other under a small bunch of mistletoe. Brent gave Eliza a look as if to say, "Uh oh." He didn't mean for Cody to get so attached to him, and, like Philip next to him, he figured the boy had accepted him into the family as an uncle, though the thought didn't upset him as much as it did Eliza and her sister.

Eliza spoke up to bring normalcy back to the day, "Cody, why don't you open some presents now?"

The boy didn't need to be asked twice; he immediately went back to the tree and began unwrapping his presents, thoroughly excited with his new drawing pencils, notebooks, and a new portfolio holder, like his aunt had.

After all the presents were opened, Mary made her way into the kitchen to start breakfast and asked for Eliza's help. Once in the kitchen, Mary began lecturing Eliza on the picture Cody drew and the relationship between her and Brent. "He expects your teacher to join the family; you know that, right? I don't want him to get hurt!" she said in hush tones so that the men in the living room wouldn't hear her.

"Neither do I!"

"Then you need to tell Cody that Collins is going away after today, that he's only here for an experiment and nothing more."

"Whatever I tell Cody, it'll be told tomorrow; I'm not going to ruin Christmas for him. And you're right, the experiment is over with tomorrow, and things will go back to normal. I promise!" Mary was about to say something back when Brent walked into the kitchen, startling the sisters.

"Need any help?" he asked as he handed his empty mug to Mary.

Mary took it and turned towards the sink, trying to look busy.

"No, thank you. Mary can handle this without either of us. We need to talk." And with that, she took his hand and led him to the balcony, grabbing a blanket off of the sofa on her way out and shutting the door.

Cody and Philip looked at each other, kind of shrugged their shoulders, and then went back to the remote-control car that Philip was trying to get to work.

The teacher and student stood and stared in silence for a few minutes; Eliza wrapped up in the blanket because it was quite chilly, and she was still in her pajamas. Brent, in a sweater, didn't feel it as much. He was more concerned about Eliza and what she wanted to say, but seeing her concerned expression, he could tell this would be a conversation that he wouldn't particularly like.

Eliza tried to gain her strength to begin but didn't know how; luckily for her, he went first.

"I'm sorry about last night," Brent began, saying

whatever came into his head to smooth over the situation, yet not fully ready for what was about to come. "I guess I got carried away."

"We both did," she sighed. "Look, Mr. Collins, I..."

"Mr. Collins?" he interrupted. "...what happened to calling me Brent?"

"I don't think we should be on a first-name basis anymore. It makes us forget our positions," she replied.

"Our positions?"

Brent paused, took a shaky breath, and continued, knowing now where they stood and feeling the pain that was beginning to form in his heart. She was reverting back to the person she was; she was pushing him away, just like she did with every other relationship that came across her door. He knew the relationship was wrong, that it shouldn't be tried, but that didn't stop him from starting to have feelings for this young woman. And now she was dividing them, and he couldn't bear it.

"I'm sorry, okay? I'm really sorry. I kissed you, and I'm sorry. I have feelings for you, and I'm sorry that I do!" he angrily said. "I can't help the way I feel! But here you are, pushing *me* away like you always do to anyone who gets close. You refuse to let any man near you feel anything because you fear that maybe things will change and be better than you ever imagined they would be to begin with!"

"This shouldn't have happened in the first place!" she replied with emphasis. "I'm just trying to make things right!"

"By pushing me away, that's going to make everything right?"

"It'll start making things right."

And she fully believed it would too; if he would just go away, all of this would go back to normal; the feelings would subside like in all other circumstances, and they could go back to the way they were in the beginning, just a teacher teaching his student. And then, once the semester was over, she wouldn't have to see him ever again.

"How many relationships have you had like this with your other students?" she retorted

"I've never had a relationship with anyone like I have with you; I've never looked at anyone like I look at you; I've never opened up with anyone like I do with you; I've never enjoyed this experiment as much as I enjoy it with you; I've never kissed..." and he stopped.

They stood silent for several minutes.

"I thought you and I were finally getting along," he continued.

"We were, but that doesn't mean that we should start something more."

"What's so wrong with what we have?"

"What do we have, Mr. Collins?"

"Don't call me that!" he said with teeth clenched. His anger was growing again, and he was having a hard time taming it. The hurt was becoming more painful with every breath. *This is what I deserve for opening myself up again,* he thought.

"What? You don't want me to call you by your name anymore?" she said.

"No! I don't want you to keep me at a distance by calling me by my last name. It's Brent!"

"Not to me anymore! We crossed the line, and I think that we need a reminder of who we really are."

"But what if that hurts too much!" he released all that was in him, and tears began to make his eyes glassy.

And without thinking, she replied, speaking out of desperation, "Then deal with the hurt, just like I will!" Her heart burst as the shock of realization crossed her mind, which made tears flow, so she let them flow freely from her eyes and cried heartily.

Brent couldn't believe what he had just heard. So she *was* suffering too. This was more than he could bear, and he needed an escape.

"Look, I don't want to cause any more pain." His voice was calm and soothing, quite the opposite of what it was previously when it was just him being attacked. "So I'll just excuse myself and leave."

"You can't leave. Cody expects you to stay for dinner."

"Well, I guess that Cody will have to be disappointed for once in his life like I am *every day* of mine." And with that, he reentered the apartment and gathered his things.

He went over to Cody, who was putting drawings into

his new portfolio.

"Hey Cody," he said.

"Hi, Teacher! Look at this, isn't it c-cool?" he asked, holding up the portfolio.

"Yeah, it's really cool... Um, Cody, I want to apologize to you for..." he paused, trying to get the words.

"Why would you apologize to me? Did you do something w-wrong?"

"I did. I made you think more of me than you ought to have," he replied.

"How am I supposed to think of you?" Cody said, still more focused on his portfolio holder than Brent's words.

"Only as your aunt's teacher and nothing more."

"But...I like you!" said the boy, now looking up at Brent with those big blue eyes.

"I like you too, but we probably won't see each other again, and I don't want you to be hurt."

"We'll spend lots of time together w-when you come over again with Auntie El."

Brent looked sad. "Not anymore...I'm sorry, Cody", he said, standing up.

"Where are you going? Christmas isn't over yet," Cody said as tears began forming in his eyes.

"I have to go; there's someplace I need to be. Please understand," he replied, and he started to walk towards the door.

Cody begged him to stay and have an adventure with him. It broke Brent's heart to keep heading for the door, but he had to get out of that apartment; he didn't want to cause any more pain or feel any more hurt. Cody began to throw a fit and cried hysterically, calling out to him.

"Teacher, please...Teacher, please, d-don't go!" but Brent opened the door and walked out.

Eliza came in after hearing the shouting, tears stained in her own eyes, and looked at Mary, who had come out of the kitchen to see what all the commotion was about. Philip tried his best to calm Cody, who had flung himself on the floor. Eliza looked down at him and scooped him up in her arms, and just held him as they cried together.

Brent headed over to the same church he was just at the previous night and walked around to the back, to the cemetery, and stood in front of his parent's tombstone and his sister's grave marker next to it, trying hard to fight the emotions that were creeping up inside of him; he'd let them loose too much lately, and he hated himself for it.

"Merry Christmas," he said, crouching down, to each of his family members, but upon looking at his dad's name, he traced the outline with his finger.

"I blew it, Dad. I tried opening myself up again, but I'm just hurting people in the process, including myself. I don't know what to do." He began to sob loudly.

He stood back up and looked around once he was done to make sure no one saw him. He needed a drink badly, he determined as his body started to shake.

He made his way back to his car and drove back to that old Victorian house, the only empty place of refuge he had. He walked into the bar area and poured himself a glass of whiskey. But as he was about to take a drink, he stopped himself.

"No!" he said and slammed the glass onto the counter.

"No more drinking my sorrows away this time." His voice rose, and he took that glass and threw it at the opposing wall; the feeling that transpired from that action was so freeing, a pent-up release, so he proceeded to break every bottle of alcohol in that bar. Every one of those bottles he considered a weakness, a hurt from the past, a new revelation that should never be. He hated the world and everyone in it.

This small act of violence seemed to free him of something, something that he didn't know quite yet. He felt better with every shattered glass, with every broken bottle, and though this room was now in a state of liquid ruin, and his hand stung with a cut that he made on one of the bottles, he didn't mind; it was nice to not be in bondage anymore.

At once, all was done, and his anger was finally appeased; he slumped down on the floor and stared at the mark on the wall where his glass hit.

"It's time to face reality… It's time to grow up," he said with a sigh of relief.

Chapter 16

The whole of next week was a lonely one for both Brent and Eliza. They tried to move on, go back to their old lives, do the things they used to do alone...but couldn't get the other out of their minds.

Brent's college friends started to come back to the house one by one, and he was not looking forward to seeing them.

He spent most of his time locked in his room now, writing letter after letter, which he ended up just balling up and throwing into the trash can. Ethan knocked on his door one day and Brent, hesitantly, let him in. Ethan examined the room and saw the full trash can with the balled-up letters.

"Is everything all right, Brent?" he finally asked him. "I saw the bar; it looks like you had a temper tantrum while we were gone. It took us almost the whole day making sure all the glass was picked up!"

"I had some anger issues that I had to deal with; I'll

admit that, but I'm better now."

"Really, then what's with the papers in the trash? Trying to write another research paper?"

"No, just…no," he said sadly.

"What happened with Eliza and your experiment?"

"I really don't want to talk about it or hear that name right now."

"Why not? What happened? I'm guessing the experiment wasn't a success like you hoped. Did she get wise to you? She's a smart woman; I always said that she was. I'm guessing that she wouldn't go along with your little game, and now you're mad at her. Did she threaten to tell the class?"

"I just need to be alone right now. Thanks for checking in on me, though. I'll see you later," Brent replied as he shoved Ethan outside his door and then closed and locked it.

Another day rolled by, and Jennifer now knocked on the door, but Brent just ignored her and went on writing and rewriting a letter to Eliza. He couldn't seem to find the right words to say to her. Nothing made sense anymore. He wanted to apologize again, but the words just kept getting all jumbled together and didn't sound right to him. An apology was all too much and too little at the same time; it didn't describe at all what he truly wanted to say. He wanted to stop hurting inside and couldn't help but think that she was probably hurting too. He wanted to drive over to her place and just hold her to let her know that everything would work out in the end. And he would have attempted it too, but for the utmost thing that was in his mind, the thing that stopped him from going at that very moment was the words that she said in their last conversation, especially what she called him, "Mr. Collins"…she didn't want him; she said that they had to remember their places. He was to be her teacher and nothing more, even if he wanted to be. That was probably what was hurting him the most.

Brent took a drive down Main Street and looked at all the Christmas lights that were still up, trying to take his mind off of his problems. He finally stopped the car in front of the bar across from the movie theatre and decided to get a drink, not of alcohol (he was done getting drunk). But maybe some water.

He walked up to the bar and took a seat on one of the stools.

"Hello, sir, and what can I get for… Hey, I know you!" the bartender said as he came over to him from helping a young couple who seemed to be on a date on the other end of the bar. "Weren't you here a couple of weeks ago with a fine honey on your arm?"

"She wasn't on my arm, but yeah," Brent replied, feeling not very sociable at the moment.

"Well, how the heck are ya! And where is your beautiful angel with the contagious smile?"

"She's not my angel; she's just my student," he replied in an irritated voice.

"Your student? How can that happen?" Brent looked at him with a face that seemed to say, "Mind your own business," but he saw that this guy was not getting the hint, so he decided to explain the situation to him and hoped that he'd leave him alone after this.

"I teach at the university, and she is taking my class. We were in the middle of an experiment when we came here," he said as he looked around the room.

"I could've sworn that you were together. You just looked so natural with each other," the bartender said as he started to clean a glass with a towel. "I thought to myself, *Self, now these two youngins belong together... how lucky can you get finding your soulmate at such a young age?* I guess I was wrong. Though I still can't get over how well you two fit together."

Brent looked down and sighed. The bartender had finally gotten the hint. He'd seen this look before. He wasn't alone because he wanted to be. He was alone because of circumstances beyond his control. He reached down and started to pour a glass of whisky that he remembered this guy had ordered the last time he was there, but Brent refused the glass and looked down again, so the bartender left him alone.

His attention went towards the couple at the end of the bar who were laughing and kissing each other quite often. Jealousy was not something Brent often dealt with, but right now, the green-eyed monster made his approach carefully towards him, and it disgusted him all the more.

He decided to get away, so he stood and walked towards the back of the establishment into the VIP room that was only lit by one overhead light that was barely enough light to see around. He sat on one of the couches and stared at the stage with the karaoke machine. This didn't help either. He began to be transported back to a couple of weeks ago. He saw a young woman singing alongside a tall, dark-haired man with many familiar features, and then he saw the bartender get up on the stage as they got down, and the young woman began to dance as she taunted the tall man. "Come on, Mr. Collins, loosen up," she would say to him. "You need to learn to relax!" She seemed to be an expert at making him do things he didn't want to do. Brent smiled as the people in front of him faded into nothing. He sat back in the barely lit room alone with his thoughts.

New Year's Eve came, and Brent spent it alone in his room while his friends partied hard down below him. The pounding music could be heard through the floorboards.

Katherine tried twice to get him to open the door, but he refused. Somehow kissing her at midnight like he usually did had lost all of its appeal, as if it had any appeal to begin with; it never seemed to have any meaning. Instead, he thought of another kiss, a Christmas Eve kiss that shouldn't have happened but did anyways. The memory made him happy and hurt at the same time because there were true feelings attached to it.

Oh, if situations were different, he thought. If they knew each other in another way, he'd be with her right now, counting down the seconds to the new year. Her lips would meet his as the world shouted their "Happy New Year." But best not to think about it now and go on with this dreary life—alone. He turned off the light and tried to go to sleep to forget this miserable existence, ignoring the shouts and music down below him.

Eliza sat next to Cody, counting down to the New Year, and then kissed him on the cheek once the ball had dropped as Mary and Philip shared a new year's kiss themselves next to them on the sofa.

"Happy New Year, Cody!" she said with a half-smile.

"Happy New Year, Auntie El! Do you think Teacher is having a happy New Year too?"

Mary stood up and looked over at Eliza; she was about to head towards the kitchen, wondering how her sister was going to handle this.

"He's probably having the best one ever!" replied Eliza with a shaky voice and tears in her eyes. She hated when he brought up Brent; it brought too many memories to her mind, and she missed him—oh, did she miss him. Cody still missed him too. Most of his pictures that week were of Brent, and no one in that apartment could get him to stop drawing him. It was Cody's way of handling the sadness; Eliza understood that, for she also was trying to handle her own broken heart. She didn't want to admit it, but she had started to care for Brent...perhaps even started to like him in more ways than she should. Why lie to herself? She knew that she did.

As Mary went to put Cody to bed, Philip came over to try to talk to Eliza, but she just stayed silent, letting him talk as she stared at the wall, waiting for him to finish, and then went into her room. She looked at the drawings on her walls, slowly examining each one. She saw the picture of Brent with the boys playing with Legos. The picture Cody drew for her for Christmas was hung next to her bed, by Cody, of course…she didn't have the heart to pull it down and disappoint him.

She went to her desk and looked at Cody's wall of drawings; most of them were of Brent now. Brent with Cody, Brent looking at the comic book with Cody by his side, Brent with herself next to a Christmas tree. It was too much. She went to her bed and flung herself onto the comforter. All of the pent-up emotions spilled out as tears onto her pillow.

Chapter 17

School started back up, and Brent walked into his class like usual, hoping to see Eliza's smiling face at her seat. The smile that he grew accustomed to seeing. The smile he longed for a glimpse to see the whole of last week. But instead of a woman, all he saw was an empty chair, and instead of a notebook, a report with a note attached to it that read:

Dear Mr. Collins,

I regret to inform you that I won't be able to finish your class.

It is for the best, though. I've learned so much from your little experiment.

And I have written a report on my findings on the topic of "fun" for you to share with the rest of the class.

Please tell Ethan that I hope he has success in his future, whatever it may be.

I wish you all the best in the world; I really mean that.

Sincerely,
Elizabeth Greene, your former student

Brent stared, shocked and disappointed at the note as the rest of his class came in. He informed them that the experiment was a success and proceeded to explain all that transpired; well, almost all, his kiss with Eliza would be kept between them. And his feelings at that moment would be kept a secret as well. Just the logistics were shared. After class, Brent packed up his bag and put Eliza's report in it to read later at home and then decided to talk to Dean Jones about Ms. Greene's absence.

"She came and talked with me this morning," said Dean Jones.

"Oh, really?" replied Brent.

"She said that due to certain circumstances, she was unable to finish your class and asked if she could transfer to another; I asked the reason for it, but she wouldn't give one, so I went ahead and transferred her to Mr. Shepherd's class down the hall."

Brent immediately left to go see Mr. Shepherd's class, but it was already dismissed.

When he got home that evening, he pulled out Eliza's report and began reading. He expected to see a bunch of negative comments, especially from the first week, but he didn't read any. She stated each event and how it felt to be in each circumstance. The only negative thing he could find was that she felt uncomfortable at his house.

Never annoyed or angry, never disgusted or disappointed (and he recalled many times that she was). She didn't even mention anything of his deceit in trying to indoctrinate her.

She gave a good review to it all and even said that she would do it again if asked. He put down the report on his desk and just sat in wonder of it all.

A few weeks went by, and Philip had had enough of his emotional sister-in-law. And, per Mary's request, he went to go speak to Mr. Collins directly and give him a piece of his mind. But when he got to the classroom, he found another young man there with red hair sitting down at the desk up front, looking at a book. The rest of the classroom was empty. Philip decided to approach the man. "I'm looking for Brent Collins. Do you know where I can find him?"

"You're not the only one looking for him," the man replied, looking up. "I came here myself looking for him too, but I can't find him. So I'm reading and waiting."

"Oh! Well..." Philip tried to think of something else to say.

"I'm Ethan, by the way," the young man said, extending his hand. "Brent's best friend."

"I'm Philip, Eliza's brother-in-law."

"Oh, you're related to Eliza! I got to meet her. She's a lovely girl, very smart."

"Yeah, we all love Eliza," he spoke quickly and with annoyance. "Look, whenever you find Mr. Collins, could you let him know that whatever he did to Eliza, I really don't appreciate it, and he needs to apologize and make things right with her, or else he'll have to deal with me?"

"What happened with Eliza? Maybe she would know what happened with Brent...he's been acting really weird since the experiment ended."

"Really? Because she hasn't been herself since that experiment ended as well."

The men looked at each other puzzled, and then a light seemed to click on in their brains. "Something must have happened between the two of them during this whole experiment," Philip began.

"Yeah, something that would cause them to become distant from people they love and care about," Ethan added.

"Are you thinking what I'm thinking?" Philip asked.

"I'm thinking that they probably had words and decided never to speak again because he's very rude and she's overly emotional."

"No, that's not what I'm thinking at all! They must've fallen in love; that's why they're acting so strange. It's the only logical reason."

Ethan ended up agreeing with Philip, though he thought that his theory was plausible too.

The men continued their conversation on how they would try to help their friends and then parted company afterward. Now knowing that love may be in the mix, they could better handle the situation. Philip went home and just told Mary that he couldn't find Collins, keeping the love part a secret for now. Mary wouldn't accept it anyway. *When she gets in one of these moods about someone, she won't accept anything logical,* he thought. Philip kept thinking into the night of ways to help Eliza. But he didn't quite know how to. So he decided to help by not getting involved, just being supportive. He learned from experience that talking to the Greene sisters was near impossible when emotions were up, and though he wanted to help her in this time of need, she most likely wouldn't listen to him anyway, just like on New Year's Eve.

Ethan was trying to write down what he was going to tell Brent. He finished a two-page letter, which he put down on his end table, and thought, *But will Brent even listen to me?* The more he thought about it, the more he realized that his words probably wouldn't have much effect on his friend, that, given the circumstances, he probably wouldn't listen to himself; his best friend was suffering, and he could only watch. So he decided to not give him the letter and balled it up to throw it into the trash can. He remembered the last time he went into Brent's room and tried to comfort him. He was, literally, pushed from the room. He was just going to have to be supportive now and wait for Brent to come to him.

Chapter 18

One night, as Brent closed his eyes to go to sleep, he opened them to an open field full of tall grass and wildflowers. The sky above was full of dark, ominous clouds, but no rain seemed to be falling yet, and there was a cool breeze blowing, which made the grass begin to dance all around him. Before him was an endless open field. He looked around but saw no one and began to run towards a tall hill to get a better view. He ran faster and faster against the wind as his legs began to ache but kept persevering up to the top.

As he approached the summit, he saw that he was surrounded by forests in the distance. All life seemed to be still and hidden, for he could not see anything moving in any direction, and yet as he made his last turn around, he saw a figure of a woman standing there alone, shivering as the wind began to have a wintery chill to it and cold rain started to pelt both of them, drenching their clothes in a freezing layer like ice against skin. Her back was turned against him and her dark hair dripping wet.

"Hello?" he called out, but she didn't seem to hear him. He walked slowly towards her and reached out his hand to touch her shoulder, but before he could do that, she turned and faced him with tears streaming down her face. Her eyes were red, and her face was flushed.

"Eliza?" he said, astonished, but she didn't answer and didn't seem to have a ray of recognition in her eyes for him. "Eliza, it's me, Brent. I'm sorry how things turned out. I didn't mean to hurt you. I just want to be with you…" He paused as the rain turned to snow; the cold chilled to the bone, and he could feel it. Her face as well began to become pale as her lips turned blue, but she made no movement to try to warm herself.

He tried to reach out and embrace her, calling her name, but his hand just went right through her like she was a projection, a shade, a ghost, and then, all at once, she began to fade into darkness and disappear.

Brent opened his eyes and sat up in bed, breathing hard as if his air had been cut off by the chill; he shivered, for it felt real; he was covered in goosebumps; it was just a nightmare—again. He looked around the room to get a sense of security that the dream was over.

Lamp, end table, desk, overflowing trash can, whiteboard…everything seemed to be in place.

His breathing slowed down, and he recovered, so he decided to try and go back to sleep. He rolled over to get into a comfortable position when he saw that he was not alone; Eliza was lying next to him in his bed, fast asleep.

"What?" he said to himself, and he went to wake her up. She woke with a start and sat up quickly, looking around.

"Where am I?" she asked.

"You're in my bed. How did you get here?" he asked.

"I'm not quite sure," she said, frightened.

He reached out to her, and to his surprise, he could touch her. He pulled her into an embrace to calm her fears and just held her like he'd been wanting to do for a while now, and she let him. "Hush now, all will be fine; we'll figure all this out...I'm here," he said to her, and she melted into him.

His heart started to beat faster as thoughts began to surface in his head, and feelings began to stir again. He decided to throw caution to the wind and open himself fully to her now. He leaned down to her and lifted up her chin and began to kiss her like he did once before. She put her arms around him to show him that she received and welcomed the movement. Neither of them had any intention of letting go as the kissing began to intensify with a burning passion.

All of a sudden, his bedroom door slammed open wide, and he broke away and looked up, startled to see a horrible figure of a skeleton of a man in a cloak. He looked a lot like the grim reaper, floating there with his arm extended, but Brent just riveted Eliza closer to himself.

Then she started to disappear from his touch.

"No!" he screamed. "Don't go, Eliza; I need you!" But she was gone. The man in the cloak remained.

"Who are you?" he demanded loudly with a determined air.

"Who I am is of no consequence," the personage said very coolly in hissing tones as if it was really a snake under that ghastly apparel. "I'm here only to make sure you don't forget your place, Mr. Collins." Brent looked at him with fear in his eyes. This was his nightmare, the one he'd seen over and over again ever since he was eighteen.

"You see, you don't deserve a woman like Eliza," the apparition continued. "You don't deserve anyone. You are alone and always will be. Do you think a good woman like her would want a broken drunk like you? Would you ever subject her to the horrors your life has become?"

The spirit began to get closer to him and pointed a boney figure at his face. "You are mine, and I plan on keeping it that way. Better forget the girl. She can't help you now, and you refuse to do anything to help yourself. So just embrace your life how it is because it will never change!" he said and disappeared.

Brent woke with eyes wide, heaving. A knock at his door scared him as he said, "W-Who's there?" with a shaky voice.

"Hey, are you okay, dude? I heard you shouting from down the hall." Brent breathed a sigh of relief as he heard Sly's voice on the other side of the door.

"I'm fine, just another nightmare."

"Okay, man, just keep it down; some of us are trying to get our beauty sleep," he said and then left.

Brent sat up and rubbed his face. What had just transpired? Had he completely lost his mind? Dreams in the past were all about him or his family. This was the first time he had dreamt about Eliza. What could all this mean?

He then slowly looked down next to him on the bed, wondering if she was there like before; perhaps he was dreaming again. It felt so real holding her and kissing her just minutes ago. Would it happen again? But no one was next to him this time. He truly was awake now. This was the worst nightmare he had ever had.

The words of the cloaked man seemed to repeat themselves in his ear. He got out of bed, turned on a light, and sat at his desk. He began to write down all that it said while it was still fresh in his mind. The last words stuck out to him, though. "She can't help you now, and you refuse to do anything to help yourself." What could he do to help himself? He wondered as the sun began to rise over the horizon.

Eliza woke up, sweat dripping down her face, soaking her pillow, and her breathing was very heavy. Tears began to form in her eyes. What had she just dreamed? She thought it all over again in her mind: Being woken up in a strange bed by Brent. Being held in his arms in a strong embrace. Having his lips gently touching hers again as they did on Christmas Eve and then seeing a ghastly figure in a cloak that seemed to make Brent uneasy and then waking up here all alone. She turned over and cried into her pillow when her door slowly opened.

"Are you okay, Auntie El?" said Cody.

"I'll be fine, sweetheart. Just go back to bed," she said softly.

"Did you have a bad dream? I have those sometimes, and they s-scare me, but then I think of you and Momma and Philip, I begin to feel not so scared. Though whenever I try to think of Teacher, he d-doesn't appear. That makes me sad. But then you hold me and tell me everything will be all right, and then I'm b-better." He paused and then looked at her tear-stained pillow. "Do you want me to hold you and tell you everything w-will be all right?" he asked.

Eliza was about to tell him no and to go back to bed. She wanted to deal with this alone, but her voice betrayed her, and without thinking, she said, "Yes."

He came over to her, climbed into her bed, and gave her a big hug. Then held her. "Hush now, all will be fine; we'll figure all this out...I'm here!" he said this familiar phrase to comfort her, but it only reminded her of being in Brent's arms, and she held Cody closer and cried again.

Cody remained with her for the rest of the night and ended up falling asleep in her arms.

Eliza, on the other hand, couldn't find sleep, didn't want sleep. The dream she had felt too real to her; it was as if Brent was actually with her, holding her and not wanting to let her go, as if something celestial was going on like her soul was searching for its other half and found it in the night while she stubbornly refused to look for it in the day. She shook her head and tried to forget it; her heart hurt too much to continue thinking about him like this.

The sun began to rise as the beams entered into her bedroom by the way of her window, the golden light dancing on the carpeted floor and the pictured-covered wall. She heard movement outside her door and thought to herself, *Time to start another day.*

Chapter 19

The next two months flew by. Winter was becoming a thing of the past, and spring was on the horizon. The flower buds were already out of the ground, and the smell of fresh grass was the fragrance that filled the air. The bird's song came back after the winter hush, and new life was seen all around.

Brent attempted to see Eliza every day since he learned of the transfer but was never able to, as Mr. Shepherd's class was at the same time as his and was always let out before the bell rang. One day Brent let class end early just so he would be there when Mr. Shepherd ended his, and he made it just in time too. But as the students passed him on their way out, Eliza wasn't a part of the group. So Brent went in to talk to Mr. Shepherd, who was cleaning up his teaching materials.

"Hello, Troy," said Brent courteously

"Well, hello, Brent. What brings you all the way down to my neck of the woods?" replied an average-height, middle-aged man whose hair was receding, and his beard started to have white intermingled with the dark brown strands. He wore glasses over his blue eyes and talked with a kind, gentle voice.

"Do you have a student by the name of Eliza Greene, by any chance?" Brent asked.

"I used to."

"Used to? What happened? I thought she applied for a full semester."

"About a month ago, she approached my desk after class and told me of an opportunity that came up; she needed her degree and promotion immediately in order to seize it. So I told her that she'd have to take the final exam a few weeks early, and I didn't think she would do well without the classes. Do you know that she ended up proving me wrong? She asked for a week to study, and when I gave her the exam, she passed with flying colors. Wasn't she your student?"

"Yes, but that's beside the point. What opportunity came up that she had to graduate early?" Brent said in concern.

"Why did she want to leave your class, though? In the whole time I've been in this school, I've never heard of anyone transferring out of your class, maybe someone transferring into it but never out."

"What opportunity, Troy!" Brent said, losing his patience; irritation was found in his voice; all he wanted was a simple answer, and this man in front of him seemed to prolong giving it.

"I believe she said that a rental came up off of Baker Street that she needed to obtain." That was all that needed to be heard, for Brent started for the door in a hurry.

"Wait! What happened between the two of you?" Mr. Shepherd shouted, but in vain. Brent was gone.

Brent took off in his car for Baker Street. He pulled up to a business complex there and saw a sign in the window of one of the buildings that made him stop short. He parked into the nearest parking spot, got out of the car, and started walking toward the building. He read the sign in the window again, "Cody's Room coming soon."

He tried the door, but it was locked, so he looked into the window and saw a classroom set up with many artistic materials, easels, aprons, and desks.

She's starting a school, he thought.

Our wise professor was only partially right; Eliza had gotten her promotion and was able to acquire the room on Baker Street, but it wasn't a school as much as an after-school club for autistic kids to teach them how to be creative, Cody's idea. The slogan was "Teaching the autistic to be artistic." This would be Eliza's side project that she could use to give back to her community and a special present for Cody.

The gentleman from the nursing home's words came back to Brent at that moment. He remembered his warnings about "the good girls" and also about how special Eliza was. And he was right…about everything. Brent could finally admit that he had fallen in love with her, and all his thoughts were consumed by her smile, her laugh, her smell, her touch…and that kiss. He thought of their past conversations and the pain he felt every time he did things that reminded him of his dad and decided that before he could even attempt a relationship with her, he needed healing from the pains of his past. He wasn't about to try for another relationship with the chip on his shoulder like he did with Jennifer. This relationship he wanted to work, so he got back into his car and drove down the street.

Eliza sat in her new office at work as her employer walked in.

"How are you adjusting?" he asked.

"Great!" she said. "The team I'm in charge of is wonderful. I'm just having a problem with Charles' confidence."

"Yeah, he's got low self-esteem, that's for sure," he replied. "But how are *you* holding up?" he continued after a while.

"What do you mean?" she asked.

"You just seem a little out of sorts ever since college, and I've been worried about you."

"Don't be. I'm fine," she said, trying to sound confident, even when she knew that she was far from being fine.

"Okay," he said. "If you say so, but I'm not convinced, just so you know. And maybe one day I'll figure you out enough to help."

She laughed as he walked back out the door, still concerned. But the smile quickly faded as she walked over to look out her window, which had a perfect view of the university. She began to wonder how Brent's class was going at that moment and if he was thinking of her as well.

Daren walked in at that moment with a bouquet of roses and set them down on her desk.

"So I hear your man is out of the picture," he said.

"Who told you that?" she asked in a low voice, trying to cover up the sadness she felt inside.

"A very reliable source. No one can look as sad as you and still be deeply in love." He came over to where she was standing by the window and put his arm around her. "I'm here whenever you need to talk."

She looked at him through the corner of her eye and began to get her sassiness back. "I really don't know what you're talking about. I'm doing great. And I'm in more love now than I have ever been in my life!" (She wasn't lying either. She finally was accepting the fact that she had fallen in love with her professor. And she wasn't about to let anyone take that away from her until she figured out what to do with it!)

"Really? You seemed single," he said, a bit disappointed, and moved away from her.

"Well, you're wrong. I'm quite taken."

Daren finally left her and went back to his desk while Eliza went back to hers. She looked at the roses and smiled as she picked them up and threw them into the trash can. She sat down and continued her project, feeling a bit proud of herself. She may still feel alone, but at least she could still keep Daren at a distance!

Chapter 20

Brent arrived at Callaway Christian Church and walked around to the cemetery like all other times before. He crouched down in front of his dad's tombstone and began to talk to him, "Hi, Dad, I'm trying to figure things out. I had the worst nightmare of my life the other night, and I can't shake it. I just see it repeating itself over and over again. I feel helpless; there's no hope for me, is there? I want to change, but I don't know how or who to talk to. It's just hopeless." He lowers his head and sighs deeply.

While deep in thought, a man approached him. "Hello, Brent," the man said. Brent looked up surprised; the sun was in his eyes, and he could barely make out who was addressing him at this moment. "Who are you?" he responded to the figure.

"I'm here to help. I overheard your conversation, and I want to help you get back on your feet."

"How could you possibly do that?" Brent tried to stand up and get a better view but lost his balance and ended up falling over onto the grass.

"I know of someone."

"Who?"

"Pastor Pike; he's helped many people that have been overcome by grief."

"How do you know that that's what I'm suffering from? Look, I don't need judgment. I get that from everyone around me," he spoke defensively. "And church people are the worst. They think they're better than everyone else, perfect little Christians. How could Pastor Pike possibly help me? He'll just condemn me for my life choices. I know he will. No, I'm not going into that church!"

"Is Eliza this way? Does she condemn you for not living a sinless life? Does she think that she's better than you?"

Brent thought for a few minutes and said softly, "No."

"Don't assume. You said you wanted help, and I'm here to help you. I won't judge you like you say that others have, and I know that Pastor Pike won't either. Now, go into the back door; Pastor Pike is currently walking towards the front of the church to gather his notes from Sunday's sermon. He will say the words that you need to hear." The man turned and walked away. Brent kept his eyes on him to see where he went, but it seemed as if he vanished as he approached the woods behind the cemetery. "That was weird," he said to himself as he stood up, having perfect balance now, and walked towards the back doors of the church.

Once inside, he saw the pastor up by the pulpit just like

the man said. He walked up the aisle and sat in the front row, silent, and stared at him. Pastor Pike looked up to see what the movement he heard was and walked over to our professor. "Is there anything I can help you with?"

Brent hesitated a moment and then began, "I-I was told to come in here; I was told that you could help me."

"Why don't you tell me what it is you need help with?"

So Brent began to tell his story about his past, the hurt he felt upon his dad dying, and the anger he had towards God. "I've had a troubled past, and I feel it's screwing up my future," he said after he had finished.

"I see," the pastor said. "And what do you want to do about it?"

"I want to fix it; I want to walk around without feeling broken and empty inside. I want to be able to love and be loved without any baggage from the past coming to haunt me!" The pastor nodded but said nothing. "Is there a way to heal me, or am I a lost cause?"

"No one is ever a lost cause," he finally said. "And I know how you can be helped, Brent."

Brent looked at him, confused. "How do you know my name?" he asked.

"I know who you are; I knew your parents long before you were born. They were married here, you know. I dedicated you when you were a baby, and I performed your mother and sister's funeral after they passed away. I watched you come here with your dad as you grew up, and I also saw when you stopped coming when you were fifteen and tried to figure out life on your own. Your dad always had me say a prayer for you. I never stopped, you know. I continued to pray for you even when your dad died a heroic death, and I continue still. It brought joy to my heart when I saw you return and sit with Eliza Greene and the Lees. They're a good family. If you want to heal, Brent, you know who you need to talk to. He'll hear all you have to say, and He will heal you. I'm only His messenger."

"Will you help me?" And he did.

He began with the most desperation that was buried deep inside of his soul; he let it all out, the frustration, the anger, the bitterness, the disappointments, the hurt. It all came out, first in awkwardness, for he had not prayed for quite some time, then in anger, as he rebuked God for taking his family away. He brought up relationships and friendships that suffered from this disease of grief that he just couldn't bear alone anymore. Then passion arose as he spoke of new feelings that he didn't want to let go, acceptance, friendship, companionship, love. All by one woman that he refused to give up. A longing that he would never let go.

He prayed like he had never prayed before. He was a broken man and poured out his soul with tears streaming so quickly down his face they would soak up an entire box of tissues.

The pastor heard every word and then prayed over him once he said amen. For the first time in Brent's life, it felt like a weight was finally lifted off of his shoulders; he felt free.

They continued to talk late into the evening. The pastor told him of a great grief counselor he could go to that would help him continue to get the healing he needed and even offered to go with him if he didn't want to go alone.

Brent left that evening feeling peaceful and in harmony with himself, a feeling he hadn't had before, and he liked it. He decided that he would set up counseling sessions first thing in the morning.

He began to smile to himself as he imagined the cloaked man from his nightmare slowly vanishing from the back of his mind. This would be the start he so desperately needed. Whether he'd end up with Eliza, he didn't know, even though that was what he desired; he was going to get better, and that made him happy all the same.

The next day he called the counselor and set up an appointment for that evening, and then he started packing up everything in his room at the party house into boxes and made several trips to his car. On his final trip, he decided to tour the house one final time; he was going to have a fresh start, and cutting some ties to the past was just what he needed to do it.

He stopped by the library, which was his favorite place to be, and was astonished to see Ethan studying something that wasn't a comic book.

"So what's the interest now?" he asked him.

"I'm studying to become a teacher."

"Really? I thought you already went down this road

before."

"Not like this. I want to be able to teach autistic children like Eliza's nephew. Ever since I talked with her that one evening, all I could think about was how she was able to teach him to write and draw, and looking at that drawing of his…"

"That's nothing," Brent interjected. "You should see the other stuff he's done," and with that, Brent reached into the box he was holding and pulled out the comic book that Cody gave him for Christmas. "He made this for me, though I haven't read it yet," he said and handed it to Ethan.

Ethan read it silently with amazement and said, once he was done, "Wow, he must really like you!"

"How can you tell?"

"Because this comic is all about you…see?" And he showed the book to Brent, flipping through the pages. He stopped on the last page and pointed to the last picture on it.

"It looks like he wants you to be with Eliza too."

Brent looked at the last picture; it was Astro Boy smiling at the teacher and a beautiful woman kissing under the mistletoe. Brent sighed. "I've hurt that family so much. I don't know if I can rectify it…" He gave a pause. "But I'm going to try!"

"I know that Eliza's your student, but are you considering asking her out?"

"She's not my student anymore."

Ethan looked at him, shocked. "What happened?"

Brent went on and told Ethan all that had transpired in the last few months, leaving nothing out, even the kiss on Christmas Eve…it was all out in the open now; he wasn't hiding anymore.

Ethan just smiled at him and congratulated him on opening himself up again to someone other than himself; he even forgave Brent for kicking him out of his room and staying away from him all this time.

Brent smiled back and congratulated Ethan, too, on deciding on a career and let him know how proud he was of him.

Brent put the last box in his car, took one final glance of the house, smiled at the thought that he was moving on, and drove off down the road.

After thirty minutes, he arrived at a house just outside of town that was next to a creek.

He opened the car door, stood up, and stared at a small cottage-style white house with green trim. Ivy was growing up on the side, and it reminded him of pictures he saw of cottages in Ireland. Memories began flooding into his brain of a family that no longer existed to him. The tire swing was still up on the tree in the front yard; the lilac trees next to the house were starting to get buds again that would bloom into the loveliest shades of purple flowers with the sweetest fragrance in another month. Hydrangea bushes lined the front windows with blossoms that would be of blues and purples soon as well. This place was turning into the prettiest place that Brent had ever seen in years.

The pain in his heart began to sting again, and all instincts told him to flee, but he stood his ground; he wasn't going to run anymore. He went up the path to the house and put the key in the door. *This is a new beginning, a fresh start,* he thought as he entered into the house that he grew up in and hadn't been into for the past three years. He was going to sell it but didn't have the heart. He rented it for a while but hadn't had a tenant for the last three years because he decided to board it up and leave the past in the past. Now, he needed to face it. He put down the box on a table in the living room, went to the window, and opened the curtain to let the sunshine in. Dust particles flew everywhere as he realized all the work that needed to be done first before he could put his plan into action.

Chapter 21

Eliza and Mary stood looking around the newly rented schoolroom. Eliza had been looking more and more serious as the weeks, no months, had gone by, and it hadn't escaped Mary's attention as she looked at her sister in dismay.

"Do we need to talk?" she finally asked.

"About what?" Eliza responded.

"About you. About what has been going on with you these past few months. I'm always here when you need to talk."

"I'm fine! Do you think this poster should go on this wall or that one?" Eliza responded, taking a poster to the opposite side of the room, trying to change the subject.

"You can't avoid me forever, Elizabeth." She always called her Elizabeth when she was trying to be motherly to her. "And you can't bottle up your emotions; it's not healthy."

Eliza went over to the big picture window and picked

up a paintbrush and stared at it.

"I'm fine," she said again, almost in a whisper. Her face grew sad. She didn't want to reopen the door of the heartbreak that she had nailed shut within her soul. "I'm fine," the lie she continued to tell herself. The only comfort she had that could stop the tears from flowing freely from her eyes and down her face. She hated being so distant from everyone, but she wanted to deal with this alone. She knew what Mary would say anyways: That she didn't think Mr. Collins was worth crying over. That it was better that he was out of their lives and she would be so much better with someone else.

"There's someone at my office that is really sweet; you should go out with him," Mary had told her one day at home. "You two have so much in common, and he loves to ice skate! If you want, I'll arrange an outing for the two of you."

"No, thank you. I'm not looking for a relationship. Never really was to begin with." And Eliza meant it too.

She wasn't looking for someone to love; she never wanted to let a man get so close to her. But what happened with her and Brent couldn't be helped. He irritated her, angered her, and argued with her. But when she tried focusing on these aspects to rid her heart of all the strong feelings of attachment, she would begin to remember his smile when she would tease him, his patience with her when she would talk for hours on end about work or Cody or anything else that came into her mind. She also remembered his words of wisdom when he did speak and his soothing, deep voice. He was a very smart man, like Ethan had said, and he didn't try to belittle her in any way. Every time she would say something of importance, he would look at her amused, almost like he was taking it all in and storing it in his brain to think about it later.

She had learned to love his hard expressions and his serious face. But she loved his laugh and smile even more. He grew when they spent time together. He went from an egotistical, arrogant fool to a kindhearted, soft-spoken, goofy prince. And she couldn't stop her heart from leaning towards him. If only she could talk to him, they could work it all out.

No, he probably hates me right now and wouldn't see me even if I begged, she thought.

On a Tuesday evening, Eliza went to the nursing home to see Arthur. She sat with him playing checkers but didn't say much and didn't smile at all.

"Are you all right, peanut?" he asked her.

"Yes, of course. Just have a lot on my mind; that's all."

"No trouble at work, I hope."

"No. Work's great. The promotion is working out very well."

"It's not Mary or Cody, is it? Or her new husband...I keep forgetting his name...Steven?"

"It's Philip, and everyone at home is fine."

"Your car hasn't died, has it? I know it has been bothersome to you."

"It's still running—your move," she said, pointing to the checkerboard.

"Well, if it's nothing I mentioned before, then it must be your teacher friend. What's his name again?"

"Mr. Collins. And I don't want to talk about it."

"Ah, so it is about him." Eliza gave him a hard stare. "What do you call him?" he continued to ask.

"What? I call him Mr. Collins. He was my teacher, you know. I was taught how to show respect."

"Yes, you were. But I heard you call him by another name the last time he was here."

"Brent," she said with a tear in her eye. She wiped it away, sat up straight, and became serious. "I don't want to talk about it," she said again.

"Oh, but I think you do. You are so broken inside, and you're trying to patch up the cracks with a type of tape that is losing its stick. Those tears need to be let out, or you'll have a flood on your hands inside of your soul, sweetheart."

With these words, the floodgates finally opened, and Eliza cried loudly and long.

"Oh, Arthur, I'm so heartbroken. I don't know how to get it to stop! The worst of it is I think I broke his heart too…no, I know I broke it. I hate myself every day. I hate everything I do. I could've…I could've…" But she couldn't go on, so overcome with emotion.

"I understand. You must love him an awful lot to be

this way."

"Exactly! I fell in love with him. That's the center of all my problems. I wish I could just go to him and tell him how I feel."

"Why don't you?"

She looked at him, broken. "Because he'll never see me. He hates me," she said.

"He doesn't hate you, peanut. He loves you too."

"How could you possibly know!"

"Because I know that young man like I know myself. He loves you and almost admitted it to me the last time he was here."

"Well, he *did* love me. He doesn't love me now," she said as she began to cry again.

"You won't know until you ask him. Go to him, darlin', and let his own words speak to your soul."

Eliza calmed herself to think of his words; she knew the truth in them. He was right. She walked over to him and kissed his cheek. "You are a very wise man, Arthur."

"Could you say that a little louder, sweetheart? I'd like old Buzz to hear you!"

How could she resist a giggle to this? She squeezed him tightly and then headed off in her car towards the Victorian house that she disliked so much.

When she arrived, it was very dark and quiet. No one was blearing music. No one was smoking on the front porch. Eliza knew that everyone wasn't away because spring break was over, and this was very weird.

She walked up to the door and rang the doorbell. It slowly opened, and Katherine stood on the other side.

"What do you want?" Katherine said with a snarky attitude.

"I want to see Brent. Is he at home?"

"You should be calling him Mr. Collins, little girl. He was your teacher, you know." Eliza took a breath and tried very hard to not revile against Katherine at that moment.

"I would like to see Mr. Collins, please," she said as politely as possible.

"Well, that's better. He's not here."

"What do you mean he's not here? Where is he?"

"He moved out. I haven't seen him in weeks."

"Do you know where he moved to?"

"If I did know, I wouldn't tell you, prick."

"Why do you call me that? What did I ever do to you?" Eliza said very seriously, trying not to get angry.

"Because you are one small, close-minded, goodie two shoes, prick. And I wish you never came here. Brent used to be mine whenever I wanted him, but now he wants nothing to do with me, and I blame you. Now, go away and don't come here ever again!" Katherine shouted and slammed the door in Eliza's face.

"Don't worry, I won't, and the feeling is mutual!" said

Eliza, and she stormed off back to her car.

She drove back home, taking deep breaths to calm herself down. She parked in her favorite parking spot and just sat there as she reflected on all that had transpired: Brent was gone, and she didn't know where he was. School would be out within a couple of months, and she couldn't make it over to the university anyways because of work.

Oh, how unfortunate all this was to find someone and fall in love only to be separated, perhaps, forever. *Well, it's probably for the best,* she thought. *He probably doesn't want to see me anyway; I've hurt him too much. I've broken his heart. He hates me. Now I just need to get over all of this...of him. Time heals all wounds; let's see if it will heal mine!* She sighed. The only good thought that came from this whole ordeal was that Katherine was upset by it; she loved that he wasn't being used by her anymore; he even moved out because of it. *Bravo to him!* She continued in thought, *I hope that he enjoys life from now on.* The thought took away the pain for a moment, but depression sunk back in as she felt loneliness creep in all around her. She eventually made her way back up the stairs into their apartment and into her room and shut the door. She thought of new plans now, plans to move out herself and away from this state.

Chapter 22

A few weeks passed. Brent was getting his counseling and was finally all settled into his parents' old house and decided it was time to talk with Eliza.

He needed to tell her how he felt, how she consumed all his thoughts every day, how he wanted to become a better person because of her, and how much he loved her…really, truly loved her.

He drove to her apartment complex and went up the stairs to her apartment and knocked on her door. He smiled and was breathing heavier when the door opened, but the smile started to fade when he saw Mary standing there before him.

"Is Eliza home?" he asked.

Mary, who was very surprised to see Eliza's old teacher standing there, hesitated a minute, wondering what he could possibly want with her now.

"She's not here!" was all she answered and began to close the door, but Brent stopped it.

"Wait! I know you're probably still upset with me, but I'm sorry, I really am…and I want to make things right. With Eliza, Cody, and you. Please, I need to see her! It's important," he said desperately.

"You know that because of you, she's planning on leaving?" she replied. "For as long as I have known Eliza, it's been her and me, and then I had Cody, and we were all that we had in the world. Philip joined our little group, and we were content and happy, and then you show up and mess it all up. Cody is sad, and Eliza…Eliza refuses to talk to me; she's keeping secrets, and now she tells me that she thinks that she needs to be on her own. I blame you for all of this!" Anger bore in her voice and rage in her eyes. She hated this man with a passion, more for what she feared had happened than for actual fact, though.

"You're right; I screwed everything up. I do that a lot. But I'm trying to make everything right. So, if you would, please forgive me for interrupting your little family; it was unintentional, I assure you. My family died a long time ago, and I wasn't used to being a part of something like what you have, and I liked it, maybe too much, but I did. And I've hurt you. I'm sorry, and I ask for your forgiveness." His genuine, complete honesty moved Mary; his countenance was sincere, and she felt that he was in earnest.

"I forgive you. But that doesn't change the fact that she's moving!"

"I didn't realize this, but if I could just talk with her, maybe I can change things. If you would just give me a chance, I'll try to get your sister back to what she was before I entered the picture."

"You really think you can?"

"I can only try," came his answer with authority and passion, as if he was resolved to fix everything like a repairman in a shop. Mary sighed and answered, "I really don't know where she is; she left here about a half an hour ago but wouldn't tell me where she was going."

"Thank you!" he said, trying to keep disappointment away, and started to run back to his car. He would search to the ends of the earth to find his love, to seek his soul.

Philip came up behind Mary once he left.

"He's in love," he said to Mary as she looked at him.

"No, that's impossible. A teacher can't fall in love with his student; that's against some sort of law, right?" she said.

"Not to my understanding, dear. And besides, he's not her teacher anymore."

She looked at him as she realized that he was right. "I wonder what's going to happen now," she questioned.

Brent searched everywhere for Eliza, visiting places that she frequented and places they went to together, but she was nowhere to be found.

He looked at the nursing home and asked Arthur, but he hadn't seen her since yesterday when she made her weekly visit. He looked at the movie house, but it was closed until later that evening. He looked at the skating rink, but she wasn't there. He even went to the church, but it was empty.

He finally decided that he needed a walk. He parked the car and got out to walk around the neighborhood, feeling a bit depressed that he wasn't able to tell Eliza how he felt and wondered if he'd ever see her again.

He walked for a while and ended up at Jefferson Park and stared at the sign; he then continued his walk in the park, passing the swings that he and Eliza sat on one evening; recollections filled his mind, and he continued down the long trail through the woods. At the end of the trail, he started to hear the familiar music of Kyle's band in the distance, and it brought back memories of months ago. He remembered Eliza's look of delight as she listened to the music for the first time. He remembered how she felt in his arms when they danced backstage and her smile that told him that she was enjoying herself.

He looked into the crowd of people, hoping to see her. Many people were there this evening, more than he'd ever seen before at a performance. Flaming Strings was becoming popular, and Brent was proud of his friends for their success. Almost all of his friends now were excelling in something that they were trying to achieve, and he loved that he was able to see and encourage them and be a part of their success even when he wasn't successful himself. But as he looked around at all the faces there, he was disappointed once again, for the face he so desperately wanted to see was nowhere to be found.

He was about to turn around and walk back up the trail

when all of a sudden, he saw someone dropping from a tree near the stage and landing on the ground; the person stood up and brushed off some leaves from off of their shirt and dirt off their pants. Brent's eyes are riveted on the figure, hoping to at last see his love. As this person slowly turned and looked up, Brent rejoiced, seeing that it was, in fact, Eliza.

She locked eyes with him too and smiled. He couldn't hold onto his excitement any longer and took off running towards her; he didn't want to take a chance of her leaving or disappearing again. He approached her very quickly and, without saying a word, began to kiss her with a long, passionate kiss. He never wanted to let her go ever again. Eliza returned his kiss with just as much enthusiasm, wrapping him into a tight embrace. She had assumed that he hated her, but she was thrilled to see that he missed her too. All the hurt and pain that had festered the last few months slowly melted away. She had him, and he had her, and they would always be there for each other.

They finally broke from each other and laughed. He smoothed her hair while looking at her face. "I love you" was all he could think to say. She was so moved by this declaration that she went and kissed him again. As she broke away this time, she answered that she loved him as well and had for a while.

He took her hand and began to sway with the music. Happiness had finally found them, and they were determined to stay like this as long as they could.

The concert ended, and everyone cleared the area. It

was just them now, so they began to talk about everything. Brent, with his revelations, and Eliza, with her burdens, were comforted and encouraged by one another and had never bonded so well in all the conversations that they'd had together up to this point.

That night they walked back to her place and as they opened the door, Cody, upon seeing who came in, ran up to Brent as he kneeled down to receive the huge hug that he never expected to receive ever again. Brent was finally accepted and loved for who he was.

Chapter 23

One year and six months later...

Brent Collins was preparing for another school year. He opened up his class as always with a greeting, expectations of the new school year, and a discussion of the great social experiment.

"In a few months, I will choose two of you to conduct this experiment, and afterward, you will each give a report on your findings. I will determine who will participate in the upcoming months," he said as he concluded his class. He quickly gathered up all his teaching materials when a student came up to talk to him.

"Didn't you used to choose one student to do this experiment with you?" he asked.

"I used to, but things are different now, and I don't do the experiment myself anymore. I have other things to occupy my time. So I choose two students to do it instead."

He grabbed his bag and exited the classroom once all

his students were gone.

He got into his car and drove down the road, passing the nursing home and the old church with a smile. He avoided the road that went to that Victorian house he once called home and continued down the main road towards the edge of town.

He drove up to Baker Street and stopped in front of Cody's Room in the business complex there. Inside the window, he saw Ethan showing one of his students how to properly hold a pencil. He was one of the best teachers Eliza had ever hired (though he was still acquiring his degree), and he loved his job with all his heart. Ethan looked out the window and saw Brent and waved; Brent waved back, smiling happily at his old friend. He had never been prouder of him as he was now. Then he continued to drive down the road.

He ended up at his little cottage next to the lake. The weather was crisp as ever, and the leaves were hanging onto the last colors of summer. The old tire swing was still there, swinging in the breeze. There was no prettier place than his little cottage in the woods. There was something new, though, a tree that wasn't there before that held a plaque that said, "Always Remembered" (it was a memorial for the family that no longer was there). A young willow but strong; it would hold up no matter what storm would come through, just like him now.

He parked in front, climbed out of his car, and hurried his steps to get inside. He set down his stuff on the table next to the front door and looked around. The living room was beautifully clean, with fall decorations on the mantel and above the entryways. No more cobwebs around or dust on the furniture. Magazines covered the coffee table, and a box of toys was in the corner. Above the fireplace was a beautiful painting of the mountains, and in the center of the mantelpiece, a portrait that Brent adored of a bride and her mate. This house was now a home, and it brought happiness into his heart to see it.

He headed to the kitchen, where he found his lovely wife standing next to the counter with a baby on her hip and a phone up to her ear; she was looking into a crockpot at the dinner that was cooking in it all day. He came up behind her and kissed the back of her neck.

"I'm sure you'll be fine giving the presentation tomorrow," she said over the phone. Brent took his young daughter out of Eliza's arms and kissed the little one's cheek.

"Charles, you're the best person I know to give this presentation. You've been at all the meetings and know more than I do at this point. You'll be fine!" she gave a few more encouraging words to her coworker and then hung up the phone to spend time with her husband.

"Everything all right?" he asked her.

"Yes, just giving Charles a pep talk. He always gets so nervous before talking to a client!" she told him.

"Are we still on for tonight?" he asked.

"Uh-huh. Mary and the boys should be here any time now," she said and gave her husband a proper welcome-home kiss.

"How was the first day of school?" she asked, stirring the contents of the pot.

"Same every year," he said

"Not every year," she teased.

"You're right. There was this one year when a certain student caught my eye and turned my world upside down. She never would let me forget her."

"And she never will!" As they shared yet another kiss, someone knocked on their door. Eliza went and opened it to see Mary, Philip, and Cody standing on the front porch. "Right on time," she said to them and started to grab her purse as they came in. Brent handed over their daughter into Mary's capable hands.

"Don't worry, we'll take good care of her," said Cody.

"I know you will," replied Brent, and then he took his wife's hand, and they headed out the door.

Cody looked up at the baby in his momma's arms. "It's time for Astro Boy and Cosmo Gal to go on another adventure, right Annie?" he said to the smiling baby.

She cooed a reply.

Brent took Eliza to a scenic overlook that looked over the whole town. It was beautiful all lit up as the stars were beginning to make an appearance in the sky. The sun sinking into the horizon made the sky turn radiantly into colors of pink and orange with cotton candy clouds. Brent turned off the motor and turned up the music. He opened his door and made his way over to the passenger side and opened the door.

"May I have this dance?" he asked.

"You know you've asked me this before."

"I know, and it worked so well the first time I thought it would work again now."

"You're so charming," she said as she took her husband's hand.

He led her in front of the car and began a slow dance to the song playing from the car.

Flaming Strings were starting to catch on as their first CD played over the speakers. As the music played, Brent remembered Kyle and the guys playing several different venues, trying to get noticed. He saw them signing their first record deal with an agency in town; the picture hung proudly on the wall in the new house that they share.

And now he saw Kyle on one knee nervously waiting on a reply from his proposal to Jennifer, who, after a bit of teasing, finally accepted his hand.

He remembered Katherine and how angry she got when he announced his own engagement to Eliza.

"How could you fall in love with that prick?" she asked him.

Brent knew the jealousy of his friend but didn't show any sympathy for her, for a few weeks later, he saw her walking down the street with her arm around a new man that he had never met.

She probably grieved for all of two seconds, he thought.

Eliza also had her own flashbacks. She remembered coming into work after Brent and her became a couple with a huge smile on her face and her spirits lifted. Her boss congratulated her and gave her a big hug; she knew he was very worried about her. She told him everything now and what she went through; Daren overheard the whole thing from the other room.

"I knew you didn't have a man! I just knew it!" he said boastfully.

"Well, I do now," she replied.

He didn't fully believe her until the company picnic, where Eliza showed up on Brent's arm. From time to time until her wedding day, he would check to see if he had any chance still, to which she'd smile and say, "Nope!" He came to her wedding, along with all of Brent's friends, except Kat!

Mary surprisingly and lovingly welcomed Brent into the family. Cody didn't need any convincing. He ran up to Brent and held him tight. "Now we're a family!"

And then there was their daughter, Annie Jane Collins (named after both of their mothers). Eliza remembered seeing how nervous Brent was as he held her for the first time. It was as if he was holding a porcelain doll and was afraid to break her. She used to peek into the nursery and watch him staring at the baby as she slept in her crib, making sure that she was still breathing and that everything was okay. He was a great dad. She felt protected and loved by him, and no one in the world had made her feel this way before; her heart would skip a beat every time she thought of it.

Brent gazed into the dark eyes of his lovely wife as they danced and thought of how fortunate he was. So entirely lucky to have this angel in his arms who actually loved him in return. She wasn't what he was looking for, but she was what he needed, and he was forever thankful to God for bringing her into his life, for turning his world upside down and healing him from his past.

"You've always caught my eye," he said, and she looked up at him. "But it was your spirit that spoke to mine, and I've been the happiest man ever since. I love you, Mrs. Collins."

"And I love you, Brent!" she replied and kissed her husband under the stars.

The loneliness was gone. The hurt and depression ceased. He found his peace and happiness in his new family. He found his healing through forgiveness and his hope in God. Eliza had helped him in more ways than he could have ever imagined, even more than she probably ever realized, though he told her constantly.

Eliza held her husband tight. She couldn't imagine her life without him in it now, and she continually thanked God in heaven for having her go back to college and into Brent's class. She felt healed herself and no longer put walls up around her, refusing to let others get close. She loved being a part of people's lives, and the town around her embraced it. Cody would always be a part of her, but he wasn't all that was a part of her.

Though romance was something she wasn't looking for and love was something you read about in books, now she was the recipient of both. She smiled up at him; this was her future, her destiny, and she knew that they would never be alone again.

The end.

CPSIA information can be obtained
at www.ICGtesting.com
Printed in the USA
BVHW051120290522
638420BV00007B/121